THE LAST TEN DEGREES

JEFF LARSON

The Last Ten Degrees
Published by Escalante Publishing
Phoenix, AZ

ISBN: 978-0-578-77750-4

Science Fiction / Hard Science Fiction

Cover and Interior design by Victoria Wolf, wolfdesignandmarketing.com

ESCALANTE
PUBLISHING

Fiction disclaimer:
This book is a work of fiction. Names, characters, places, and incidents either are the product of the author's imagination or are used fictitiously, and any resemblance to actual persons, living or dead, business establishments, events, or locales is entirely coincidental.

To Barbara, my beautiful wife, for her unending love, support and encouragement.

STONE'S TRAVELS

COLORADO

NEW MEXICO

UTAH

ARIZONA

NEVADA

CALIFORNIA

Santa Fe

Albuquerque

Gallup

Lake Powell

Page

Flagstaff

Tucson

Phoenix

Kanab

Fredonia

GRAND CANYON

Williams

Lake Mead

Las Vegas

Needles

Colorado River

JULY 6, 2036

STONE LAB
LA JOLLA, CALIFORNIA

AIR TEMP 101°F, 8:00 A.M.

THE SUN HAD COME UP one and a half hours before as Jeremy Stone, MD, PhD, stood looking to the west toward the Pacific, sipping his coffee.

Dr. Stone, a fifty-two-year-old genetic scientist, was the owner of Stone Laboratories in La Jolla, just north of San Diego. A Nobel Prize winner, he had received many grants from the National Institutes of Health in genetics and cell biology over the years.

The lab had been built in 2014 at a cost of $25 million, half of which had come from wealthy donors in San Diego and Los Angeles who were interested in his research. The facility was quite large and was designed in two main sections with the latest architectural design.

One section was strictly for research and the other for production of biomolecules. Most of the research section had nearly floor-to-ceiling windows and allowed the staff of thirty, many of whom were MD-PhDs, to get incredible views of the Pacific Ocean. They used the latest in robotic assistants to help with experiments. A white board that floated in front of each of the researchers allowed him or her to play with experimental algorithms by voice command.

As Stone looked to the west, from the third story of the building, he could see construction cranes moving some of the beach houses farther to the east, away from the ocean's edge. Others were being placed on stilts. This had become necessary as climate change had heated the oceans, and water levels around the world had been rising alarmingly since 2015. In 2025, a huge chunk of the Antarctic ice sheet had broken off and melted, raising sea levels by two inches. In 2027, the Greenland ice melt in the summer had accelerated to such a degree that it had precipitated another two-inch rise in ocean levels. Coastal cities had begun building dikes to counter this effect, but the water had continued to rise.

World freshwater supplies were decreasing, but some cities, like San Diego and Los Angeles, had anticipated the future shortages, had built desalinization facilities, and had begun to use purified wastewater. In fact, San Diego's two desal facilities now supplied roughly 75 percent of the city's needs. Other major cities, such as

Phoenix, had not been as wise and had delayed construction of further water-supply facilities. As a result, these cities lacked an assured water supply and suffered the consequences. In these areas, their water had become increasingly scarce, and out-migrations to other parts of the country had further diminished the resources and capital necessary to address this problem.

As Stone looked to the south along the shore, he could see one of the two desalinization plants gleaming in the morning sun. It supplied the northwest part of San Diego, and Stone's lab was included in that area.

Looking again toward the ocean, something caught his eye. He could just make out several dark shapes floating near one of the construction cranes. They seemed to be bobbing at the edge of the ocean.

Stone grabbed some binoculars and saw that the shapes were, in fact, three humpback whale carcasses. They looked to be quite bloated and dark in the morning sun. They had attracted a crowd of beachgoers, who stood there gawking at the creatures, covering their noses from the smell.

Since the ocean temperatures had risen to new levels, several marine species, including whale species, had begun to sicken, and in some cases, completely die off. The die-off started with coral reefs, then advanced to include more species: several types of fishes, marine lobsters, dolphins, and then whales. In fact, the whole migration of these humpbacks had changed. Normally at this time of the year, they would be much farther north, near Alaska, but now they were being washed up on the beach at San Diego.

As he watched, Stone could see a large environmental cleanup crew begin to remove the whale carcasses from the beach. This had become a distraction for the many tourists coming to enjoy San Diego's beaches. And whale-watching tours had folded years ago, in 2025.

After finishing his coffee, Stone went back into the lab to talk about the morning's research with his close collaborator, Chris Sorensen, PhD, the Head of Research at Stone Laboratories. Sorensen had worked closely with Stone for almost fifteen years. Sorensen oversaw the PhDs, postdocs, and MD-PhDs in Stone's lab. On most mornings, Stone liked to go over the day's planned research with him.

Sorensen was Stone's top man in the lab and had even shared the Nobel Prize with Stone in 2024 for deciphering the smallest genetic sequence capable of coding for a living cell. Sorensen was a brilliant scientist who enjoyed doing difficult biological calculations in his head, sometimes baffling the other scientists with his mathematical quickness. He had obtained his PhD at UCSD in three years in cell and mathematical biology at the young age of twenty-two, then spent three years at Scripps Research Institute for his postdoc. Later, Stone chose him to work in the lab in La Jolla, where he quickly rose through the ranks, first as a senior scientist, then working closely with Stone on some of his most exciting and challenging experiments. Stone enjoyed working with Sorensen because of his exceptional intelligence, his math ability, and his ability to problem-solve the most complicated experiments.

Stone had been involved since the 2010s in researching the secrets of human and animal genomes, including how DNA is translated into RNA and how the genes were turned on and off by two little types of RNA called miRNAs and siRNAs (for micro RNAs and small interfering RNAs). In 2015, Jennifer Doudna, PhD, had pioneered the use of CRISPR technology. Suddenly it became possible to modify tiny sequences of animal and plant DNA at will. The Chinese had even experimented on human embryos in 2018, which had shocked the world. The United States and the European Union had quickly banned CRISPR use in human embryos, but the Chinese had forged ahead with the technology and in 2026 were even experimenting with enlarging the muscles of young men destined for their two-million-strong army. Along the way, there had been successes and failures, as the Chinese had experienced trouble repeating the exact changes from one embryo to another. As a result, larger muscles developed in the adult army men, but other unwanted effects were also present, such as strange facial features, large noses, and small ears. Nonetheless, the Chinese had gone forward and now boasted the strongest army in the world.

Stone's main interest was deciphering the molecular secrets of DNA and RNA and how the cell controlled the transcription and translation of protein. The basic process of transcription had been decoded shortly after James Watson and Francis Crick in 1957 had found the structure of DNA. What followed was the beginning of molecular biology, and labs since then had homed in on these molecular processes.

Stone's work in the 2010s had focused on trying to describe the simplest machinery necessary to produce a replicating cell. He had coauthored a paper with Sorensen describing this research in 2022. For that, they had won the Nobel Prize in 2024. Since then the science of nanotechnology had captured Stone's fancy. Scientists at Harvard and other American universities had shown, at least theoretically, that it might be possible to create molecular-sized machines capable of almost any function, relying on their tiny size and unlimited ability to create and process other molecules.

In the early 2020s, scientists had perfected a virus capable of injecting a gene directly into cells of the retinas of patients with retinitis pigmentosa, thereby almost curing them of the disease. Their night and peripheral vision had been 90 percent restored. This success had not been lost on other PhDs who were engaged in trying to genetically engineer cures for other diseases. In 2022, scientists at the Pasteur Institute in Paris had designed a nanomachine that had for the first time shown promise in potentially improving or curing type 1 diabetes. This had been the Holy Grail of diabetes research for fifty years. The nanomachine was actually a specific combination of nanomachine and genetically modified virus that attached itself to pancreatic cells of diabetic patients and reprogrammed the cells to start producing insulin. Modest success had been achieved with this, and a few patients had gotten along on much reduced insulin for at least five to ten years or had not needed insulin at all.

All sorts of money had been thrown at this new nanotechnology, and Stone's lab was no exception in receiving it. Stone, since winning the Nobel in 2024, had used the award money and money from his other novel organism patents to expand on his interest in nanotechnology research. He had made rapid progress in designing a nanomachine capable of treating cancer cells, first in mice, then monkeys, and later, humans. Stone had forged ahead into the human cancer arena, designing a nanobot potentially capable of attaching to and treating human lung cancer. In the early 2030s, many types of solid cancer tumors had been successfully treated with newer drugs or other therapies. However, lung cancer had remained exceedingly difficult to treat. Thus, Stone's research was part of the final frontier in lung cancer research.

The idea was basically this: A large number of nanobots (hundreds of millions) would be injected into lung cancer patients' veins. The bots would quickly track through their blood streams and home into the patients' lungs, where they would track down the lung cancer cells, attach themselves to the cell surfaces, and then inject a synthesized peptide into the cancer cells. The peptide would interfere with the cancer cells' ability to repair their own DNA by inhibiting a DNA-repair enzyme. Because the DNA would not be repaired properly, the cancer cell would not be able to continue into the next stage of the cell cycle, the division stage. The very mechanism of the cancer cell that allowed it to continuously divide would be halted. Thus, the cancer cells would be selectively destroyed.

This cancer nanotechnology had been tried some years earlier, but there had been problems with the machines attacking normal cells. The early peptide molecules had also been less effective. Now, in 2036, these problems had been solved.

The nanomachine that Stone designed was constructed in a special factory in La Jolla near his laboratory. The size of the nanobot was astonishing. It measured a mere 25 nanometers wide (1 nm equals one billionth of a meter).

The nanobot consisted of a temperature monitor and a drug chamber that contained the necessary peptide. The nanobot's carbon/lipid nanoparticle membrane was designed to fuse with the cell membrane of the cancer cell after binding to a specific surface molecule.

In the 1990s it was discovered that cancer cells, and

tumors in general, maintained a slightly higher temperature than normal cells. This is because tumors are generally supplied with a higher density of small blood vessels, and the tumors secrete chemicals designed to attract the increased circulation. With more blood vessels entering the tumor mass, the temperature of the tumor is raised significantly, in some cases by 1.5 to 2 degrees Fahrenheit. The bot was designed to inject the lethal peptide when the slightly higher temperature of the cancer cells was sensed.

The binding energy for lung cancer cells versus normal lung cells was much higher. Thus, the bot would preferentially bind to the cancer cell and eventually kill it.

It wasn't a perfect system, but in Stone's lab, they had shown a kill rate of 94 percent, an unbelievably large percentage. The 6 percent of the tumor that remained would then be easily destroyed by the body's own immune system. It was the first time that this type of nanosystem had worked well in experimental animals, and it was ready to be tried in humans. Stone would soon be traveling to Denver for the phase III human clinical trial. He was racing against other labs that were also on the doorstep of perfecting the technology.

Meanwhile, Sorensen had personally overseen the final preparations of the experimental nanobot. Stone himself would personally deliver the bot to a hospital in Denver. Stone had spent a lot of energy on these nanomachines, and he was extremely paranoid about their being discovered by a rival lab, so the plan to carry the machines personally made good sense to him. He was also afraid of flying and afraid that he might catch another corona virus. They had finished the last production series of the nanomachines, enough for the clinical trials, in the second week of June 2036. The trial was to take place at Banner West Hospital in Denver and would be overseen by an old friend of Stone's, Dr. Marc Casper, Director of Research at the hospital. Stone and Casper had previously worked together during one of Stone's postdocs at Scripps Research Institute, and afterward they had followed each other's careers with great interest. Now, Casper had offered to shepherd the phase III trial of the bot. Stone and his lab stood to profit immensely if the nanobot succeeded even modestly in treating lung cancer in humans. Money had already been raised from Stone's many backers, some of whom were scientists interested in his work. The Denver phase III trial had occupied almost all of Stone's and Sorensen's time and energy over the last several months.

As a result of the importance of this project, Stone and Sorensen had planned to package the experimental nanobots in two places in Stone's luggage. The experimental machines had been split up between his briefcase and his travel pack, both of which he intended to carry with him at all times on the trip to Denver. Stone had insisted on separating the bots into two separate containers in his luggage to ensure that, even if one piece of luggage was lost or stolen, he would still have enough machines for the experiment.

Now, as Stone finished discussing Sorensen's morning research, he listened to Sorensen describe the plans for the Denver trip.

"Jeremy, I think we're ready for the trip now. Just remember that we'll be separating the nanomachines into two groups. One group will go in your briefcase and the other group into a travel pack. Both groups will be cooled to within 1/8 degree of 38 degrees Fahrenheit to preserve the nanomachinery and the surface coating and binding proteins. I know you'll be going through some incredibly warm areas on your trip, and we don't want any unnecessary internal heating in these things."

"Yeah, I know. I just looked at the forecast for the next ten days, and it looks like it might hit 128 or 129 when I get to the Grand Canyon."

"OK, and remember to keep the bot cooler inside the Super Prius and out of the sun. The cooler is programmed to handle fluctuations of as much as 45 degrees, but I don't want to take any chances."

"OK, I'll be careful."

"Don't spend any more time than you have to on this trip. I know you want to take some travel photos with your new wide-angle 3D lens, but the phase III trial is almost ready to go in Denver. I just spoke to Casper, and he's expecting you in nine days."

Sorensen then went over the two cooling machines,

each of which was powered with a tiny nuclear generator. Each was no bigger than a small cup. Yet each would hold approximately 200 billion nanomachines in a state of neutral electrical conductivity. They were floating in a special chemical formula that would be kept at the precise temperature of 38 degrees Fahrenheit.

Stone grabbed his briefcase and travel pack and headed out onto the deck of the research facility. Sorensen followed with his suitcase. Several of the lab researchers came out onto the deck to send him off. It was a beautiful San Diego day—air temp 101 degrees and ocean temp 86 degrees. It would be good to be on the road and away from the lab, a luxury Stone rarely allowed himself. He placed the travel pack and briefcase along with his suitcase in the travel storage compartment and climbed into the Super Prius.

The Super Prius was modeled after the Teslas of the mid-2010s, and like them, had four separate electric engines at each wheel. With its newly designed lithium-silicon battery, it could reach eight hundred miles on one charge. Top speed was a whopping 165 miles per hour, but Stone rarely had the opportunity to drive it that fast.

Stone didn't mind taking a major road trip by himself and excitedly looked forward to the time alone. His ex-wife was also a PhD, an Alzheimer's researcher whom he had met at Scripps during his postdoctoral research. The marriage had proceeded nicely through the postdoc years—until Stone's penchant for younger women got the best of him. After he'd had several affairs with female postdocs, his wife divorced him. Except for the occasional fling, Stone had been directing most of his energy to the research, sometimes spending most of his nights in the lab. He still found himself attracted to younger women and had enjoyed two affairs with younger scientists, but these hadn't lasted long. Lately, he didn't have time for affairs and was almost completely consumed with the nanomachine project.

Jeremy had chosen a path from San Diego to LA, through Needles, on through Williams, Arizona, to the Grand Canyon, to Kanab, Utah, and then southeast to Page, which held the Horseshoe Bend of the Colorado River. He chose these spots for their photographic beauty, and they promised to give him time to test out his new wide-angle lens.

He set the inside temperature of the car to 69 degrees, voice commanded the computer to chart a course of least traffic north out of San Diego, and hit the start button. He cruised north on the 5 through Oceanside, where he saw surfers riding high waves, and went by the big Marine base at Pendleton. Just then several H60s screamed overhead. They were the latest in marine jet aviation, with a top speed of Mach 2.4 and boasted two nuclear-tipped missiles, each with a range of 150 miles. The jet noise startled him, and he briefly lost control of the car, but the Super Prius self-corrected instantly.

As he drove along the beach west of Pendleton, he could see off to his left where the military had erected dikes to prevent the rising Pacific Ocean from inundating the large base. Many coastal cities had erected these types of barriers to keep the ocean water from flooding their low-lying areas.

In spite of worldwide attempts to contain fossil fuel emissions, the CO2 reading on top of Mauna Kea in 2036 read 678 parts per million. The ocean level rise had followed this continued rise in CO2.

Stone planned to stop briefly at Caltech in Pasadena to look in on some experiments that one of his former postdocs was completing. Her experiments had probed how lung cancer cells turn off the immune system's attack by cloaking themselves with an unusual protein. This research might help him when he got to Denver and began the phase III trials on the nanobot.

Just north of the Marine base, Stone saw the sign for the San Diego-LA "Tube," an underground magnetic transport tube that ferried traffic at high speeds between the two cities. Some called it the "Musk tube" in honor of its inventor, Elon Musk. By voice command, Stone readied his car to enter the tube. Computers took over from there and whisked the Super Prius along at 320 mph. It took only twenty minutes to reach the outskirts of the big city.

Entering south LA, coming out of Musk's tube, the car flicked on its lights, reacting to the thick smog. LA had a population now of 20 million and maintained its dubious record for dirtiest city in the US. Ozone and small particulate levels exceeded standards at least 290 days out of each year. He took the Pasadena freeway north and drove on to Caltech.

Sheila McCafferty, PhD, was waiting for him in her lab. Sheila, thirty-two, ran a lab of three other postdocs and two senior scientists that had been funded by Caltech and the NIH for several years now. She was happy to show off the lab to her former mentor, who now beamed like an expectant father. As he smiled, his eyes took in her shape and beautiful eyes.

"Great to see you, Jeremy."

"Likewise. Fill me in on the latest."

"Well, we isolated the cloaking protein last week and are in the process of sequencing it now. We'll know in a few days how it works."

Stone was always happy to see that the postdocs who had trained with him were making new discoveries. In this case, Sheila had been one of his top trainees, and he, of course, felt as though her accomplishments would reflect positively on him. Unlike some of his other trainees, with whom he had had affairs, he had let Sheila alone to pursue her research.

"That's excellent news. I'm heading up to Denver to start on a phase III trial with one of our nanobots, and we may be able to use your results."

"Great, I'll keep you posted. I can text you when we get the structure.

"We're planning to test the protein in a lung cancer culture system first and go from there."

"Excellent. Give my regards to your other lab members, Sheila."

"OK, Jeremy. Safe travels!"

Stone walked back to his car in the Caltech parking lot and then headed east through the smog on the 210 by the San Gabriel foothills. He noticed quite a few bare hillsides and some huge dry mudslides that had come to rest near the highway after the record-breaking fires in 2032 and 2034. Four hundred sixty families had lost their homes, and seventy firefighters had lost their lives.

After Rancho Cucamonga, he took the 15 north through Victorville and began the climb up to the high desert and Barstow. As he passed the east side of Edwards Air Force Base, the car was shaken briefly by a loud sonic boom from some research craft. He had heard that they were testing a new hypersonic fighter.

As the pressure wave hit the car, it veered slightly to the right, but the onboard computer corrected quickly, and within seconds the car was back on track.

At Barstow, he stopped briefly at a roadside date place. He purchased a date shake. The coolness felt good against his tongue and refreshed him from the outside heat. The outside sensor read 125°F. He checked the readings on the bot cooling machines. Everything was nominal. After Barstow, he took the 40 east toward Needles and listened to the latest pop star sing of her regrets. His thoughts drifted back to San Diego and his lab there, but about twenty minutes out of Barstow, the computer voice announced, "Barstow-Edwards weather service: Wind warning for 4 p.m. to 6 p.m. July 6. High winds reaching 45 to 55 miles per hour and chance of significant dust reaching 87 percent. Be alert and use dust lights."

Beginning in 2030, new cars in the Southwest were equipped with high-penetration sodium dust lights. Without the lights, it could be impossible to see traffic ahead in the major dust storms that frequently occurred in the high-desert area north of LA. Stone switched on the lights as a precaution and adjusted his speed accordingly, from 110 to 70. Several brown clouds were crossing the roadway roughly ten miles ahead.

Another warning voice came on from the Super Prius computer sensor: "Dust cloud ten miles ahead. Probability of crossing highway 97 percent. Density 3.4 grams per cubic meter."

As Stone drew closer to the cloud, the Super Prius automatically decelerated for the conditions, and he noticed other oncoming sodium lights peeking out of the brown dust. The computer also adjusted for the side-winds, and after a few miles, he was clear of the cloud.

Stone pulled into Needles shortly after 7:00 p.m. He descended into the Colorado River Valley and pulled into a Holiday Inn Express. A sign outside the motel read, "Elevation 495 Feet. Gas $9.10/Gal. Water $19/Gal."

Stone parked the car, checked the cooling machines holding the bots, and stepped inside the motel. After registering, he purchased a chicken and hummus meal from the meal dispenser, went to his room, and after slowly eating the meal, fell asleep while watching the virtual TV which hung in the air above his bed.

The next morning, he spoke to the motel receptionist before departing.

"I'm planning to head east, through Kingman, and then on into Williams. How have road conditions been lately?"

"Well, if you're headed that way, watch out for forest fires. We've had some really high temperatures here, and I hear Arizona is just as bad. Just make sure you have enough water and money for charging. Our electric prices here are good because we have a lot of solar in California, but the prices in Arizona are astronomical. They're running about twice as high as here. And watch out for the water robbers. They've been seen holding up the large water tankers and stealing water from their tanks."

"Thanks," Jeremy replied. "I'll keep that in mind."

Jeremy took his suitcase, briefcase, and travel pack out to the car, where he turned the AC to high, bringing the internal temp down quickly to 73.

Stone had taken this route four years earlier on another vacation trip, and as he crossed the bridge over the Colorado, he was shocked to notice that the river's width had shrunk considerably. On that previous trip, he had noticed a multitude of tall saguaro cacti. North of Needles, the elevation climbed another three hundred to four hundred feet, an ideal elevation for saguaros. Four years ago, the hillsides had been covered with all sorts of saguaros and other vegetation, including creosote, chollas, and bursage. The saguaros at that time seemed to be all different heights, from a few inches to almost forty feet tall.

But now he noticed that in some places there weren't many small cacti at all, and the hillsides were dominated by the tall saguaros. The other desert plants weren't as prevalent either. He had read that the saguaros, like many other species, were beginning to respond to climate change. But with the higher temperatures and longer dry spells that were now occurring, the baby cacti couldn't store enough water, which was evaporating much more quickly. As a result, there were now far fewer small cacti. And the hillsides here were becoming more barren. The saguaro, a keystone species, was now beginning to fail.

JULY 7

NORTHWESTERN ARIZONA

AIR TEMP 112°F, 9:00 A.M.

AS STONE DROVE farther east past Kingman toward Williams, the vegetation became sparse indeed. He remembered that between Kingman and Williams, there had been large conifer forests, some quite dense. Now he noticed that the forests had thinned considerably, and in several places forest fires had taken their toll.

Upon entering Williams, he saw that the town had shrunk in size. Driving down the main street, he saw broken windowpanes in several abandoned buildings. A small café was surrounded by two blocks of empty store fronts. Stone noticed several tongues of mud that had cascaded down from nearby hillsides denuded by wildfires. The mud that had settled in the streets flew up and began to cover his car.

It had been an interesting drive from Needles. Outside of Needles, he had noticed some sand drifts on nearby hilltops. Here also, he saw some small dunes, mostly a brownish-orange, and the wind was picking up. He then realized he was quite tired. Several signs advertised lodgings, and he picked out a small inn. He also noticed signs that advertised the price of water: "$22/gal. The Cheapest Water Here to the Grand Canyon."

It was no secret that water prices in both California and Arizona had skyrocketed ever since the two main reservoirs, Mead and Powell, had begun to fail. But unlike Arizona, California had at least tried to conserve and augment its water supply. LA had used treated wastewater for drinking since 2014, and San Diego had gone to 75 percent desalinization.

Stone pulled into the motel. As he stepped outside the car, the heat blasted him. Normally, at 5,000 feet in elevation, Williams would have been in the 60s, but in the last four years, the temperatures had begun to soar. A thermometer outside the motel registered 114°F. He quickly picked up his bags and camera gear, registered, and after connecting the charge cord to his Super Prius, headed for his room. He was asleep by 9:00 p.m.

Next morning, he quickly showered, dressed, and headed for the breakfast bar. He chose coffee, juice, and toast as the least risky options from the simple breakfast bar. A virtual TV blared the news. As he ate breakfast, his eyes landed on the view from the window. Was it that smudged or was the air itself hazy? Curious, he asked the clerk at the registration desk,

"What's with the air?"

"Must be that forest fire up toward the Canyon. That's the third one we've had this year, and then the rains came after the last one, and you can see what the mud has done."

"OK, I'm headed for the Canyon today. Will there be any problem getting through?"

"Nope, don't think so. The fire's a bit to the west of the road, and I haven't had any complaints from tourists the last two days. But you never know with these fires. The winds have picked up like I've never seen them, and you know what can happen to fire when the winds pick up."

"Yeah, I remember the Koffmann fire north of Santa Barbara in 2029. That was a real mess. Some three hundred thousand acres in two days!"

"Just make sure you have enough gas and water to get where you're going. We only get a tanker here now every two weeks. And after you get to the Canyon, if you're going east and north, then there isn't much water or gas before Page."

"OK, I have an electric vehicle. Are there enough charging stations at the Canyon? I plan to spend a day there taking photos, and then I'm heading east to Cameron and then Page."

"Sure, plenty at the Canyon, but fewer east of there."

The clerk cast an eye at Stone as he paid his bill and headed out to his car. He hadn't seen many Canyon tourists lately, only a few people from Phoenix or points east, and the recent wildfires had discouraged a lot of them. He wondered how long he'd have a job, given what was happening with the climate.

JULY 8

INTO THE
GRAND CANYON

AIR TEMP 111°F, 8:00 A.M.

STONE PULLED THE CHARGE cord from the Super
Prius, paid $5/kWh, and headed north. He drove slower
due to the haze. It would have been more difficult, but
a stiff wind from the northwest cleared some of the
haze away. The car maintained the speed he set by
voice command.

As Stone got farther from Williams, he noticed a sign
off to the right near what used to be the small town of
Valle: "Air Museum Closed. No Gas for 200 Miles."

Four years ago, he had stopped at the aircraft
museum, which boasted several German World War
II planes and an old four-engine Lockheed Super
Constellation that President "Ike" Eisenhower had used

for his mobile command post in the 1950s. Now all that remained at the old museum site were some small, brownish drifting sand dunes.

Stone slowed as he approached Tusayan, south of the Canyon, because the smoke became noticeably thicker. He glanced at his outside thermometer: 112. Normally, summer temperatures near the Canyon were pretty high, but he couldn't remember it having ever been this hot.

In the 2010s, Tusayan had mushroomed into a community of summer homes and six thousand people. The governor had green-lighted development at the urging of investors who envisioned profiting from summer homes for city dwellers and out-of-state investors. Water at the time seemed plentiful enough. But then came the mistakes of the early 2020s. With the Drought Contingency Plan in early 2019, the powers that be thought they had fixed the problem of falling levels in Lake Mead. Under the plan, the farmers in Arizona were the main ones who took a hit. But cities such as Phoenix were also affected. The planners had waited another six years, until 2025, to finally begin addressing the long-term problem. By then it was too late, as the levels in the two great reservoirs were dropping rapidly. Compounding the errors, uranium miners had been given a green light also, and by 2015 it was obvious that uranium was leaking into the groundwater around the south Grand Canyon. By 2030, with the declining flow from Lake Powell into the

Canyon and the polluted drinking water, Tusayan's days were numbered.

As Stone approached the area where Tusayan used to be, he saw only abandoned houses, and again, the slow drift of sand. Approaching the Canyon, Stone saw signs advertising water for twenty-five dollars a gallon. With the diminishing flow into the Colorado from Lake Powell and the accelerating warming from climate change, water had become a scarce commodity near the Canyon. In the early 2000s, a long pipeline was built down into the canyon to extract water from the river for the lodges on the Canyon's edge. It had been repaired several times, but now there simply wasn't enough flow from the pipe to keep up with demand. The only other supply of water into the Canyon area was from the large water tankers once a week from Vegas and Needles.

Stone had a reservation for the night in the only tourist lodging left, the old Bright Angel Lodge, which had been remodeled to 150 rooms. The price had increased to six hundred dollars a night in the 2030s, a result of the lack of staffing and the high cost of water and food. In 2025, the sound of multiple helicopters ferrying tourists over the Canyon could be heard, but now only the sound of the wind competed with the soft hum of the Super Prius. Once there had even been a long tramline to carry tourists over the edge and down into the Canyon, but that had vanished long ago. Even the mules that once carried people down the Bright Angel Trail were gone, victims of the water issues and lack of tourists. Some hikers still ventured down into the Canyon, but with daytime temps in the summer approaching 135°F at the bottom, only a few hardy souls attempted this.

Stone had packed his best photo equipment for the trip, including the newly purchased wide-angle lens for the Canyon and several filters to deal with the dust in the air. Even now, a slight haze obscured the beautiful details he could begin to see below.

Stone was met at the lodge by one of only two park rangers left, Jack Morgan. Jack had spent the last fifteen years at the Canyon and had seen many changes to what was once the most-visited national park in the country. Jack sported a scraggly beard and suntanned face that belied his seventy-one years.

"Welcome to the Canyon. How long you planning to stay?"

"Well, just today, unless the haze hangs around," Stone ventured.

"Oh, so you're a photographer?"

"Well, yes. I've always wanted to capture the Canyon, and now I've got a new wide-angle lens I want to try out."

"Some of the photo seekers have tried special filters, especially when there is dust in the air."

"Yes, I know, and I have several to try today," Stone responded.

"Well, let me know if I can help. Oh, by the way, no hiking down Bright Angel today. The haze is just too thick for safety, and that fire down the road isn't quite out yet. They've had an air tanker flying for three days now, and she's only about 70 percent contained."

"OK, I'll keep that in mind. Any place a guy can get a cool drink?"

"Yeah, we have a bar on the basement level of the lodge. Nice view of the Canyon too. But the water's so expensive now that you might need a small fortune for that drink."

"Thanks."

Stone registered and put his luggage in his room. He removed the bot coolers and placed them on a nearby table. Then he locked his room and headed for the bar. It had a great view of the Canyon, despite the haze obscuring the view out over Mather Point. He grabbed a table by the large window and waited for service.

The minute he saw her, she had his full attention. This was better than watching porn. He adjusted his crotch and looked up into her brown eyes.

"Hi, what can I get you?" came the soft, smooth voice of a beautiful twenty-six-year-old with dark hair.

"Hello, what's the best beer you have?"

"Canyon Pale Ale is my choice," she said.

"OK then. Bring me a bottle."

As she walked away, he followed her lovely hips as they swayed rhythmically across the floor. She was well-endowed also, a turn-on for him. When she returned, his hard-on had calmed a bit.

"So what's your interest here, stranger?" she said, looking directly into his eyes.

"Oh, I want to try some shots with my new camera. But this haze seems to be getting in the way."

"That's too bad. Maybe it will diminish overnight."

"Yeah. Maybe. Say, where you from?" Stone asked, hoping for a friendly response.

"Oh, just down the road in Flag. I'm a master's student at NAU. My major is biotech. I'm working on some research with one of the scientists doing biodiagnostics. We're developing an array that will measure exposure to things like soil fungus and coronavirus."

"Great, I'm in research also. Who's your professor? "

"Zack Thomas. He's been there for fifteen years and has published a lot recently."

"Don't know him. Have you worked with CRISPR, PRIME, or any of the newer techniques?"

"Oh yeah. And we've got a cryo-electron microscope too."

"Really. That's impressive for NAU."

"Yep, the research has been going so well that grant money has been flowing lately."

Stone nodded. "Got to stay on top of things, or no grants will come in, and someone else may steal your results."

"Yeah," she replied. "By the way, what's your area?"

"Well, I'm on my way to Denver to begin a clinical trial for lung cancer. I've brought along some of my nanomachines to test in a phase III trial at a hospital there."

"Wow, that really sounds interesting. Perhaps you could tell me more about it later. But I've got to go wait tables some more."

"Sure. Maybe I'll see you later at dinner, and we could talk more then," Stone said with a hopeful expression.

"Good. I'm on tonight."

"OK, see you then! By the way, what's your name? Mine's Jeremy."

"I'm Sasha."

Stone smiled as she walked away.

Stone's groin responded again to the visuals, and as he finished his beer, he watched the hips move back and forth. He decided to head back to his room for a brief nap until the light was better for pictures. He awoke as the travel alarm sounded at 3:00 p.m. Looking out the window, he could see that some of the fire haze had dissipated. He grabbed his camera and filters and left for the edge of the Canyon.

The afternoon light was still a bit hazy, and he knew he was going to have some difficulty. But maybe that newest filter could help. As he screwed on the filter, he saw only three other tourists at the Canyon edge. Four years earlier, the place had been swarming in July.

He positioned himself along the edge of Mather Point, being careful to secure the tripod and give himself enough room. He aimed the wide-angle toward the west, where the sun would set. The pale walls of the Canyon shone back at him in the afternoon sun. As he looked farther down into the Canyon, it was astounding to realize that the five thousand feet in depth represented some 1.8 billion years of history.

He decided to try five or ten shots at different angles to the sun, thinking he might come up with two or three good shots. Stone had always been a perfectionist when it came to science, so this part of his personality came through as he made his practice shots. He took at least five or six minutes to position the camera for each shot, painstakingly adjusting his tripod as he went. He calculated the exposures in his head, as he did almost all of his lab calculations. Math had always been easy for him, and several advanced math courses near the end of his PhD had added to his capabilities. Even so, Stone also had an artistic side. He could appreciate a beautiful photograph of nature as much as a well-thought-out experiment. And here at the Grand Canyon, he was really enjoying the experience of being outside and trying to capture the best photos.

The sun was getting lower to the horizon, and he had to adjust his filters to counter the rapidly reddening light. After a few more minutes, he watched the sun disappear behind the Canyon rim, so he went back to his room to review the day's work. He scanned quickly through all the photos and was glad to see two or three that perfectly captured the quality of the light he was after.

Sasha was there when he entered the dining room.

"Hi again," he said as he took his table. He was happy to see her again. The fast-setting rays now barely illuminated the Canyon, and the yellows and oranges from earlier in the day had now turned to purple and grey.

"What do you recommend?"

"Well, we have a special tonight of Apache trout. They used to fish them from the Canyon in the old days, but then the water became too warm. They import them from Albuquerque now."

"Sounds great. And bring me another one of those beers too."

"Sure. And I want to hear more about your research."

"No problem. Happy to tell you about it."

"Great. I get off in about half an hour. How about I come back to your table, and you can clue me in?"

"Excellent, I'll be waiting."

Stone enjoyed the trout and his beer. He was still working on the key lime pie when she returned. He felt his body react again to her presence.

As she sat down, he again admired her brown eyes and short dark hair.

"So, what do you want to know?"

"Well, tell me more about the nanomachine!"

"OK. Another scientist and I have been working on it for about four years. It's passed phase I and II trials in San Diego, and now I'm taking it to Denver for phase III human trials. It's been shown effective in the animal models and is predicted to have a 94 percent kill rate for human non-small-cell lung cancer.

"Wow! Quite an accomplishment! How does it work?"

"I can't give you complete details because we haven't fully patented it yet, pending the human clinical trials, but I'll try."

Her eyes widened with interest as he began to explain the research.

"First, they're tiny: each is twenty-five nanometers wide, and we're going to release about several hundred million into each test subject's veins. They're all adults between forty and sixty-five with non-small-cell lung cancer who have failed radiation, surgery, and chemo. I'm traveling to Denver because one of my old colleagues in my postdoc is now chief of research at Banner Denver West, and he's agreed to have the trials in his hospital. NIH approved also."

"So how does it work?" she repeated.

"The basics are this: It has a receptor for the cancer cells, and then the machine will inject a synthetic peptide that will block the cell cycle, so the cells can't divide, in effect killing them. The whole thing is triggered by a temperature receptor that will selectively recognize the higher cell temperatures of the cancer."

"OK, so what else can you tell me?"

"I'll tell you what. Come back to my room. Let's have another beer, and I'll give you more details."

Sasha looked intrigued. Stone was reasonably

attractive for a man in his early fifties, but her real interest lay in finding out more about the nanomachine.

They walked quietly back to Stone's room. Stone opened the door.

Sasha thought for a moment. If this ends in sex, I've done this before with other professors, so no big deal.

Stone said, "Come on in. I'll order room service for two beers. OK?"

"OK. Just let me use your bathroom for a moment."

"Sure."

Sasha went into the bathroom. She thought long and hard. Maybe a little tease will get him interested, and he'll reveal more information. It could be helpful for her career since it was still difficult for women to advance in the sciences. She quickly pulled the soft blouse off her chest, revealing her beautiful cleavage.

As she stepped back into the room, Jeremy was calling room service. As he put the phone down, he caught sight of the perkiest breasts he had ever seen.

"Hope you like this," she said softly.

He was startled for a moment at the sight.

"Ah, yeah . . . but I thought you wanted to know more about the experiment?"

"Well, I thought there would be plenty of time for that." She now positioned herself on the edge of his bed.

"Tell me, Jeremy, are you married, or do you have a girlfriend back in San Diego?"

"Ah, no . . . not right now." Stone's face began to blush

slightly. "I've been divorced for a while. Been too busy in the lab lately for anything else."

With that, Sasha got off the bed and drew closer, and he felt something growing larger in his crotch. He was hooked.

She loosened his belt, pulling his trousers down. His erect cock stood out at her like an invitation. She dropped to her knees and began sucking, just like other times with her professors. Those times had led to promotions in the lab. This time it might lead to getting more information from Stone.

After a few minutes, Stone couldn't stand it and ripped her jeans off. He began to tease her nipples with his tongue. They stood out like little cherries. Sasha moaned. As he finally entered her, her moans grew louder. First, he pumped her quickly on the bed, but she became more excited and asked for more. He rolled her up on the edge of the bed and penetrated her again. As he grabbed her breasts, her excitement only grew. Her hands grabbed the edge of the bed as she came multiple times. Finally, Stone released with a loud yell, "Oh baby!"

The two of them collapsed on the bed.

Further explanation of the little nanomachine would have to wait.

The next morning, satisfied with his photographs and the sex, Stone dressed and ate a quick breakfast. Sasha was already on duty in the restaurant and said, "Jeremy, it was so great to be with you last night. Here's my cell

number. Let me know how your research turns out."
He responded positively, loaded his gear into the Super
Prius, and headed east out of the Grand Canyon area.
His next driving objective was Fredonia and The Wave.

JULY 9

NORTH CENTRAL ARIZONA

AIR TEMP 111°F, 8:00 A.M.

STONE WANTED TO TRY his luck in the lottery for The Wave, a geologic feature well-known for beautiful sandstone layers of varying colors that dated all the way back to the Jurassic. It required a half day difficult hike to reach. Stone had entered the lottery six months previously but wouldn't know until the day he arrived whether he would be one of the four hikers allowed in the following day. As he headed east out of the Grand Canyon tourist area, he again noticed the drifting layers of sand that occasionally covered the road.

When he hit US 89, he turned and headed north toward Page. Almost immediately, he came upon the tiny town of Cameron, which in the past was regularly visited by scores of buses sporting tourists from all over the world. As he pulled into the Cameron Trading Post for coffee, he noticed only one tourist bus and very few cars. It seemed that the trading post business had also dried up significantly. After coffee, turning north, he immediately crossed the Little Colorado River Gorge, which in the past held a relatively shallow chocolate-colored river. The color arose from the strata nearby. Today, he crossed over a dry riverbed with only some shifting gray-colored sand in the bottom.

Heading farther north on 89, he came to the site just west of Tuba City, where signs had declared, "Walk to Dinosaur Tracks." The Navajo used to charge tourists to view sets of three-footed tracks from the Jurassic. However, there were no signs today as he proceeded down the road.

Stone glanced at the outside temperature gauge. It read a toasty 119°. He came to the fork in the road at a town called The Gap, where one fork led east up a plateau into Page, and the western fork led to Bitter Springs, the Vermilion Cliffs, and on into the area near The Wave and Kanab, Utah.

He took the western fork and immediately saw the tall formation known as "Echo Cliffs," another geologic structure that went almost from Gap all the way to Bitter Springs. He could see layer after layer of folded Jurassic rocks, laid out in various colors of red, orange, and yellow to the right of the road. After Bitter Springs, he continued north to the Vermilion Cliffs, so named because of their pale, pastel, pink-and-bluish colors.

He stopped the car for a look and took a photo of the cliffs. Other folks also got out of their cars, but not to photograph the cliffs. They were there for the release of some California condors, birds so rare in the 2010s that only eight breeding pairs remained. At the time, they had been decimated by eating carcasses containing lead shot. Their numbers rose to almost forty pairs in the 2020s, but then the increasing temperatures on the Paria plateau had driven them down again to about eighteen pairs. Nevertheless, the ten-foot wingspan of these creatures looked magnificent in the morning light.

Stone photographed some of the birds being released and, after watching them soar into the cliffs, got back on the road. The country now turned markedly to wilderness, with strange rock and cliff formations everywhere and far fewer cars. At a scenic overlook just west of the Vermilion Cliffs, he stopped for an incredible view.

Much of the eastern course of the Colorado River was visible, as it wound in snakelike curves and disappeared over the horizon. In one area, he could see how deeply the Colorado had cut into the rock, appearing as though someone had taken a giant trowel and gouged down into the earth some thirty-seven hundred feet. He took another photo and headed toward Kanab.

At Jacob Lake, he stopped for lunch at a roadside deli and began chatting with the owner.

"I don't remember temperatures this high when I was here four years ago. And there's obviously more sand blowing in from somewhere."

"Yeah, it's different now," the owner remarked. "We've taken a hit here ever since the temps started to rise significantly, say three or four years ago. And our water supplies have become quite slim. We used to see a lot of tourists here in the summer, as we are the gateway to the north side of the Canyon, but now we have to wait to get our weekly ration of water from the tanker trucks and take whatever they have left after their deliveries into Kanab."

"I'm headed for The Wave; put my name in months ago. Do you see many hikers headed there these days?"

"No. In fact, about the only folks that visit The Wave are professional photographers from outside the US, and they've been few and far between lately.

"Still, we've hung on here, mainly surviving on the summer tourists from Phoenix and Vegas. When it's 128 degrees in Phoenix in the summer, they all flock north to escape the heat. Of course, even though we're at about fifty-five hundred feet in elevation here, we've had some real doozies lately. It hit 132 last week, and the forecast isn't much better for the rest of the month."

Stone thanked the owner and continued on his way. Five miles east of Fredonia, a small town south of Kanab, a dirt road to the right signaled the stopping point for those who wanted to wait out the lottery call for The Wave. A sign proclaimed, "The Wave—Best Jurassic Formation in the USA—Water $26/Gal. Get Your Supplies Here."

The Prius came to a smooth stop on the dusty road outside the shack where the lottery tickets would be drawn that day. Stone noticed the license plates—rental cars mostly. He guessed they were from the international tourist-photographers who had been customers at the deli in Jacob Lake. One sole Utah plate stood out among the rentals. He grabbed his camera bag and went inside.

Nine or ten people waited in line. It was 12:30 p.m., and the drawing wouldn't be held until 3:00 p.m. Some were purchasing supplies needed for the hike—dust masks, suntan lotion, hats, water, and snacks. It seemed like most people had expensive photo equipment, and Stone spied at least one wide-angle lens like his. He sat down on a nearby bench, grabbed a soda from a machine, and waited.

At 3:00 p.m. sharp, a local administrator from the Bureau of Land Management announced the drawing.

"Only drawing this week. Trail group leaves tomorrow morning at 6:00 a.m. sharp. Six point four miles round trip. Miss Crystle will be your guide. Make sure you have sunblock SPF 75, hats, and plenty of water. Follow your guide's instructions. You'll only have about forty minutes at The Wave, which should be plenty of time for photos. Weather is hot tomorrow—127 is predicted, with clear sky and light to moderate wind. Humidity will be 4 percent. By the way, you'll all need cooling vests, which we'll hand out before the hike. Without them, you'll definitely have trouble surviving in the heat. The only motels are five miles down the road at Fredonia or fifteen miles farther at Kanab. See you tomorrow."

The waiting photo-tourists all stood up.

"Here are the winning names—Loeden, Fitz-Allen, Thorsen, and Stone."

A loud "yeehaw!" traveled across the room.

After his name was called, Stone collected his ticket and headed to Fredonia for dinner and a room. Fredonia was next to the Vermilion Cliffs National Monument in northern Arizona. Entering the motel, he noticed several Native Americans registering guests and waiters serving customers. Stone registered, gulped a cool drink from the bar, and headed to his room for a nap. He carefully set the briefcase and the travel pack containing the bots on the floor. That was the last he remembered until the alarm woke him suddenly from a weird dream at 5:15 a.m. The sun was just coming up over the horizon when he grabbed a quick breakfast in the dining room. He packed his camera gear and headed for The Wave station. As predicted, the weather was clear and hot and the wind light, but he still noticed occasional drifts of soft, brown sand covering some of the road.

When he got to the station, the other three hikers were already there waiting with the guide, a Native American woman about thirty or thirty-five years old.

At 6:00 a.m. sharp the group departed the shack and headed south. The guide used her GPS for directions. The sky was clear in the area, but as Stone looked to the north-west, he could see a brownish haze beginning to appear. Signposts called out the mileage every half mile. At mile-post two, one of the tourists asked the guide to stop.

"I need to get a drink," he called in a sharp German accent.

The group rested and took drinks from their water bags.

"Where are you from?" Stone asked another tourist.

"Central England," he replied. "I've been waiting three years for this trip. I've been to Arizona and Utah before, but this is the first time I've been able to win a spot in the lottery!"

"Yeah, I feel lucky too," Stone said. "I bought a new wide-angle lens this year that I'm trying out. I took some fun shots at the Canyon yesterday. Got some new dust filters and everything. I hope we won't need them today."

"Well, I don't know," the Brit mused. "In spite of the wind prediction, it's already picking up, and when I came down yesterday from Zion and Kanab, the dust was blowing pretty hard."

The group continued on until they spied the curv-ing shape of The Wave in the distance. The formation stood out sharply from the rest of the scenery. It was indeed shaped like a giant ocean wave, multicolored and fitted with layer upon thin layer of brilliant yellow, brown, orange, and red sand. The sand had hardened into rock, having been compacted over the eons by wind and weather. It seemed almost unreal.

"OK, get your pictures now. We only have forty minutes, and the wind's picking up, so we may get some more dust later this morning," the guide yelled over the growing wind.

Stone and the others painstakingly positioned themselves for the best photos. They had spent over two hours hiking the three miles, and some of the photo-tourists were already complaining of the heat. Stone tried some different filters and exposures, always reviewing them immediately in the new camera, and was thrilled with the results. He exchanged exposure settings with some of the others, and after forty minutes, they were ready to go. The wind had reached twenty-five miles per hour and was increasing quickly, according to the guide's portable anemometer.

As the group headed back to the lottery shack, some dust began to cover the ground. The guide again relied on her GPS to stay moving in the correct direction. The sky was turning an orange-brown.

There was so much dust that the group members were told to put on their face masks. Even so, the dust particles stung around the edges of their faces and began to get in their eyes. Some of the hikers had trouble staying upright. The guide pulled out her air thermometer.

"Looks like we just hit 126 degrees. And the wind hit

37 mph. OK. At this evaporation rate, we need to take a drink every ten minutes. You're losing massive amounts of water and electrolytes from your bodies, and I don't want anyone to pass out. We've still got about two miles to go. Anyone feel dizzy or fatigued?"

She glanced around the group and noticed that the man from Britain was having trouble putting his water bag back in his pack. She went over to him and gave him an extra dose of electrolyte-rich fluid, which she carried with her. After a minute or so, he seemed to recover, although his face started to flush, turning slightly red. The guide turned to the others.

"If anyone is feeling flushed, extremely hot, and dizzy with a severe headache, let me know, and I'll give you some electrolyte fluid. You probably have heat exhaustion, which is common in these temperatures. We had a photo-tourist here last month, when it was 129, and he passed out shortly after starting back. Probably heat stroke, which can be fatal. We had to call in a helo to evacuate him to Kanab."

The group listened intently and continued its slow trek. The sky continued to fill with dust. The group made it back to the lottery shack, but it took an extra two hours. Most of them bought extra Gatorade and other electrolyte solutions at the shack and guzzled them down. The guide looked perfectly comfortable. After checking to see if they were all right, she said, "OK. Continue to drink fluids and get some rest this afternoon at your motels. Thanks for being good tourists, and we'll see you next time."

Stone climbed into the Super Prius, now covered with the orange-brown dust, and drove slowly back along the main road to Fredonia. There, exhausted, he went to his room, drank some more Gatorade, and decided to take a long nap. After cleaning the dust away, he quickly stowed his camera gear in the travel bag and fell immediately asleep.

Stone didn't wake until early the next morning. He said goodbye to some of his fellow hikers staying at the motel and headed north toward Kanab.

JULY 11

KANAB, UTAH

AIR TEMP 113°F, 8:00 A.M.

BY THE 2020S, Kanab had grown into a major tourist destination in this southern part of Utah. There were cattle farms, and some farmers grew wheat and corn, but the main business was tourist excursions. For $1,500 you could take friends or family out for four days with a four-wheel-drive vehicle into the semiarid area around the town and camp out while your guide pointed out coyotes, bobcats, and occasionally even a cougar. Multiple hiking trails surrounded the area, many leading around and up sixty-seven hundred-foot mountains that provided excellent views of the countryside.

Kanab was also the gateway to Zion and Bryce Canyon National Parks. However, after 2025, with the rising temperatures and resulting dryness, the tourist outfits in

Kanab and the parks had trouble attracting tourists. The town of Kanab had shrunk from forty-five hundred to one thousand. Most of the remaining people were either die-hard farmers or the few guides who still worked in Zion National Park, thirty-five miles up the road.

Several weather-beaten signs outside of Kanab stated, "Water $27.50/Gal. Last Gas until Bryce."

Stone pulled into a drive-in diner. A thin teenager skated up to his car, her face covered with a green bandana. She wore torn jeans and a long-sleeved shirt and carried a water pack on her back with the spigot stuck in her mouth.

"I need something cool," Stone told her.

"OK. We have electrolyte soda, electrolyte water, and iced electrolyte punch. What would you like?"

"I'll try the electrolyte punch. And make it quick. I'm dying of thirst!"

The brown wind had abated somewhat. Stone resumed his trip, heading east out of Kanab toward Page. As he made the turn east at the junction of the road that led to Zion, he noticed a large, recently constructed sign that read, "Park Closed—Rock Fall in Entrance Road and Temps Too High—All Hiking Trails Closed until Further Notice."

The sign was dated June 27, two weeks earlier. Stone glanced at his outside temperature gauge on the Prius. It read 118°F.

As he drove east toward Page on US Route 89, a new

warning light came on in the Super Prius, something he had never seen before. It was giving him an overheat warning. He had been running his AC at full blast, and it wasn't keeping up. The car's internal temp was now reading 85. Beads of sweat poured from his head. His older model Super Prius had been designed in 2028, when the maximum temperature in the western US rarely reached 115 or 116. He now wished that he had purchased a newer model. He pulled off the road and consulted his onboard computer. The computer was telling him to leave the motors off for ten minutes, check his water levels and oil levels, and then, if both levels were OK, to proceed, but at a somewhat reduced speed. Since he had just purchased the car six months earlier, he didn't want to damage the engines. Not to mention the precious nano cargo that he carried.

Stone turned the engine off with the push button and sat quietly in the car. The temp inside gradually rose from 85 to 91 and beyond. He grabbed at his beverage cooler and took a large swig of electrolyte solution. That helped, but he realized he would be in trouble if he had to wait much longer without the AC. The cooling containers for the bots could go to an internal car temp of 97 or 98, but that was about it. Fortunately, the engine light had gone off. He called the car computer, and immediately a current road map came up on a virtual screen on his windshield, showing the route and distances to Page. The robotic voice stated, "Eighty-seven miles to Page.

Eighty-seven point seven percent chance of completing trip. Twelve point three percent chance of failure in AC. Eleven point one percent chance of engine overheat."

Stone asked his onboard computer, which was named after one of the moons of Jupiter, "Io, next weather and temperature forecast for the Kanab/Page area July 11–21, 2036." The response was immediate in a slightly different voice:

"Weather clear. Temperature forecast 128 and rising by approximately one degree each day over next seven to ten days. Probability 96.7 percent. Large record-breaking, high-pressure area located twenty miles west of Los Angeles and extending east to St. George, Utah and beyond, expected to move east slowly next seven to eleven days, creating extreme life-threatening temperatures. All environmental precautions advised."

Stone contemplated his situation. He had never experienced temperatures this high. Certainly four years ago on a trip nearby to Zion, it had never gotten above 110. And that was high, considering the local elevation of 5,100 feet. His choices appeared to be these: (1) go back to Kanab or even Grand Canyon until the temperatures moderated or (2) continue to Page, risking a motor or AC malfunction, although the computer had put that likelihood at only 11 to 12 percent.

Stone thought about the nanomachines sitting in the cooling compartment in his briefcase and pack. He had planned for the storage of the bots in the cooling apparatus, but he realized that if he waited much longer, the car temps might overload the cooling margin. The experiment could be ruined before it could even start.

He made a quick decision, pushed the start button, and headed east, just below the recommended speed of 65 mph. The AC kicked in immediately, and within a minute or so, the car's internal temps dropped, and he felt much better.

The AC seemed able to maintain itself at that speed, and he heard no further warnings as he cruised along. There was sparse traffic, only an occasional car or large water tanker. Halfway to Page, Io stated, "This is the Las Vegas National Weather Service. For July 11, 2036, extreme environmental temperature warning, deserts of the near southwest. July 11–21, daily temps reaching extremely dangerous levels, 127–136°F. Travelers are advised to carry appropriate types and amounts of fluids and electrolytes, especially for longer trips. Outside excursions limited to ten minutes maximum regardless of clothing. Danger of heat exhaustion and heat stroke high. All precautions advised or avoid this area entirely for next seven to eleven days."

Stone realized that if, in fact, a vehicle emergency did occur, his likelihood of rescue was slim. This road had become relatively untraveled recently, and only one air rescue service was left in Page. Two or three air rescue companies had been in service in the late 2010s, mainly for the large number of paleontologists who came to the

Page area at that time. The dinosaur hunters wanted to dig out whatever remaining fossils they could find in the Grand Staircase-Escalante National Monument before 50 percent of the monument was taken out of protected status to allow coal mining.

In fact, during the late 2010s and beyond, fifteen new species of triceratops had been discovered in the Staircase. Many other dinosaurs had been discovered there as well, including one named for a local paleontologist, Merle Graffam, called *Nothronychus graffami*. The monument was rich in such ancient fossils, complete with T. rexes, hadrosaurs, and triceratops of the Cretaceous age, some ninety to one hundred million years ago. However, after the president's executive order, half of the area was opened for coal. As Stone glanced ahead, a sign advertised, "BLM Dinosaur Museum, Three Miles Ahead on Right. Bad Water, Five Miles."

Stone had always been interested in the early history of the earth, and his first career thought had been paleontology. On his last visit to Zion four years earlier, he had missed this museum, so now the sign definitely whetted his interest. He turned the Prius into the BLM site and immediately saw a painting of a large hadrosaur on a nearby building. The site seemed deserted. He quickly exited the car and went inside, leaving the AC on to cool the bots. Given the temperatures, he planned to make a quick stop.

Just inside the entrance he saw a large curved, black

claw that could only have come from a very large dino-saur. The caption under it read, *Tyrannosaurus rex*, Grand Staircase-Escalante, south side, 2025." He walked left into the small museum. There on one wall staring directly at him were ten or twelve triceratops head mock-ups, all looking slightly different. One sported seven sharp head prongs, another had five, and still another had only one. They were replicas of actual triceratops specimens that had been found over the last fifteen years in the staircase. He just stood there, awestruck.

"What do you think about those?" came a deep voice from behind the desk.

"I actually found the one on the left in 2014 about sixteen miles up in the staircase, in an area they are now mining for coal."

Stone turned to see a seventyish-looking, slightly disheveled man talking to him.

"My name is John, and I run the museum now, or should I say try to keep it open. Since the executive order and that damn new interior secretary, we have all we can do to keep going. But we have some of the best fossils in southern Utah. The townspeople in Bad Water tried to help us every year with their dinosaur festival and parade, and we still get a few donations from other parts of the county. Take a look in that other room. You won't find better examples of juvenile T. rex skulls within five thousand miles of here."

Stone went into the other room and saw that John

was right. Four small skulls were mounted on one table, along with other leg bones and small claws that had been found alongside them. He recognized the classic look of T. rex, with large areas of open space in the skull and razor-sharp rows of teeth in the mouth.

John followed him into the other room and asked, "So what's someone like you doing in the area? You don't look like a fossil hunter."

"Well, just passing through. I'm headed for Denver by way of Page."

"Seems like a roundabout way to get to Denver."

"Yeah, but I like the scenery, and I'm taking some photos I've always wanted to do along the way."

"OK. Hey, have you ever seen Horseshoe Bend below Page?"

"Yeah, once as a kid with my parents, but now I've got a new camera, and I can't wait to take some new wide-angles of that site."

"Be careful. They've got a huge new tourist fence. They put that up a couple years ago when they had those suicides jumping down into the Colorado, but there are still other areas that are relatively unprotected. They've got a limit on how much time you can spend there now. Some tourists still come in spite of the temperatures. I was there just last week, and I couldn't believe how many were there. Mostly rich tourists, I guess. They fly in from all over and then take the bus tours and visit the sights all over Utah and Arizona.

"And Lake Powell is a fraction of what she once was. They drained most of the lake to refill Mead back in 2023."

"Thanks for the education."

"No problem. Come back again. We only get visitors about once a week now. I'm still digging in the north staircase, but the finds are slim there."

"Well, good luck. Judging from what's here, you'll find more."

Stone climbed back into the Super Prius. The internal temperature had climbed another four degrees due to the stoppage, but Page was close now. He headed east through what used to be Bad Water. He could still read a dilapidated broken sign that read, "Dino Festival, Oct. 25–27." It was turning slowly in the wind and was half covered in dust.

As Stone headed southeast toward Page, he caught sight of the last remnants of Lake Powell and some other brighter reflections gleaming in the afternoon sun. A large water tanker had passed him when he went into the BLM museum, and it now appeared way off in the distance ahead of him. Another sign off to the left advertised, "Visitor Center, Glen Canyon Dam, Two Miles."

Stone breathed a sigh of relief that the Super Prius had held up, and he turned into the visitor center, which was located about a quarter mile up an asphalt road on the west side of what remained of the Glen Canyon Dam. He parked the car under a sun protector, left the

AC on, got out, and walked into the center. A sign gave the completion date of the dam as 1966.

A balding, older man with a green ranger's uniform greeted him. "Welcome to the visitor center, or should I say, what's left of it. I'm David Yang, lead national park ranger for the dam museum. Come on in! Would you like to hear a brief history of the dam and visitor's center?"

Stone nodded, and Yang continued.

"In the old days, the museum and visitor center were located along the west edge of the actual dam and were filled with exhibits about the dam's construction and information about the southwest watershed. You could actually look north then through the visitor center window and see the deep bathtub ring around the edge of Lake Powell. With climate change and rising temperatures, we had to downsize the visitor center and slightly relocate it. This building doubles both as a small visitor area and as a viewing office for me to check on the solar arrays farther up the lakebed. When the lake was nearly drained in 2023, a large solar company came in and created 275,000 solar arrays. They needed someone to keep an eye on them, so I signed up."

Stone glanced northeast and saw a huge area of bright reflections off the solar arrays.

"What kind of arrays are they?" he asked.

"State of the art," Yang said. "With this large collection of arrays, Arizona has become the nation's leading supplier of solar energy! We have a group of about 150 technicians on the Navajo Nation now to maintain them. They have built upon the previous transmission lines from the1960s and modernized them. We now transmit power all over the country.

"If you have a few minutes, walk around and see the exhibits we have left."

Stone spent about fifteen minutes viewing the remaining exhibits. He marveled at the construction photos from the 1960s and read about the electricity generators operating back then. The dam had produced 1,320 megawatts a day before it had stopped producing electricity.

Yang approached him again. There were few visitors that day, so he relished having someone to talk to.

"I don't know if you know this, but back in 2023, they drained most of Lake Powell. There simply wasn't enough inflow from the upper-tier states to keep the dam producing electricity. So they created two large drainage ditches around each edge of the dam and let most of the water that was left in Lake Powell flow down the Colorado and into Lake Mead. There's only about 10 percent of the lake left now. As a result, we lost a lot of the tourist business. Used to be rafts you could take down the river below the dam. We had three companies doing that back then, but they left long ago.

"Page is a ghost of what it once was. Used to be about seventy-five hundred people. Lucky now if we have a thousand full-time residents. It's hard to get water and food here for those who are left. My wife and I still live here, but I've got the two jobs to keep me busy. What did you say you came for?"

"Photography," Stone said. "I bought a new wide-angle camera and came to try it out on my trip to Denver. I already photographed the Grand Canyon and The Wave and want to try some photos here, too."

"Well, if you want some cool photos, try Horseshoe Bend. It's only a mile or two below Page, and even with the severely diminished Colorado flow, you can still take in some incredible views. By the way, if you're going beyond Page to the east, there's no water for about two hundred miles. And I just picked up the regional weather forecast for the next seven to ten days. Apparently there's an unusually large high-pressure area parked off LA that's started to move east. The temps are expected to go up quite a bit over that period."

"Thanks. Yeah, I heard about the weather coming in. I'll keep that in mind. Thanks for all your help. I think I'll head into town for some lunch. Then I'll head down to the Bend."

"OK, good luck!"

Stone got back into the Super Prius. The large water tanker that he saw earlier had vanished into Page. He glanced at the outside thermometer. One hundred and twenty-five degrees at 11:30 a.m.

The engine warning light did not come on.

He headed east across the new bridge. This had been

built after the old bridge collapsed when the drainage ditches had been constructed. At the far end of the bridge, he noticed the town sign: "Page, Arizona, population 1,015."

The old population number of 7,500 had been painted over and crossed out several times. Stone headed up the hill into Page.

JULY 11

CARL HAYDEN VISITOR CENTER AT GLEN CANYON DAM

AIR TEMP 125°F, 11:30 A.M.

AFTER STONE LEFT the visitor center, Yang opened the outside door to his office after stepping up to ground level. The light struck him directly in his eyes. He was seventy-five now, and the recent heat wave had taken its toll. He immediately covered his eyes, donned his hiking hat, and stepped outside. His office had been reconstructed several years earlier, when the temperatures started to rise on the plateau. New records were broken every day back then, and it was necessary for a new office to be constructed underground to compensate for the heat.

In his ranger's uniform, the temperature felt oppressive. He checked his outdoor thermometer and humidity gauge. At 11:30 a.m. it was 125 degrees and 4 percent humidity. He checked his cell phone, and the expected high for the day read 131 degrees.

Yang glanced across the remains of the Glen Canyon Dam, completed in 1966. The main wall, which held enough concrete to pave a highway clear across the U.S., was crumbling badly. In fact, it had been crumbling for a long time, ever since the final drainage ditches had been constructed in 2023 to allow most of the water in Lake Powell to flow into the Colorado River and then into Lake Mead. It wasn't an easy decision. But with the rising temperatures and declining snowpack that fed into Lake Powell, there simply wasn't enough runoff to keep feeding two major reservoirs.

The environmentalists at the time were outraged. They worried about the effect the drainage would have on species such as the humpback chub, a little nine-inch minnow that lived in the Colorado between the two big dams. And they worried about the trout, with declining trout catches below Lake Powell. But in the end, the climate won.

The major southwestern drought that had begun in 1999 had gone on for over thirty years. In 2021, the tree-ring specialists at the University of Arizona in Tucson had warned state leaders and the people at the Central Arizona Project to expect a much-longer-than-average drought. They could see what the climate had been nearly all the way back two thousand years by the width of tree rings in the southwest. Their warnings, however, had gone unheeded. As a result, new ideas for a desalinization plant in the Gulf of Baja to augment water supplies had been shelved, and Arizona would suffer through three major cuts on the Colorado River water. All the larger cities in Arizona had taken water hits, and the city populations had begun to decline. Farmers in Pinal County and all over the state had ceased production of water-sucking crops such as alfalfa, cotton, and almonds. Wells in Tucson and Flagstaff were nearly tapped out, creating a major outflow of residents to other states, those that were water-rich.

Yang glanced at the sides of the now-crumbling dam. Once in the beginning, in the late 1960s, it had been full. Back then, there was one major drainage port at the base of the dam that used to discharge nine million acre-feet of water into the Colorado on a yearly basis.

But that was when the rivers up north still ran full and Lake Powell filled to capacity every year. Then the snowpack began to decrease in Utah and Colorado, and the rivers that fed Powell gradually became a trickle of their former selves.

As Yang looked across what remained of the dam, he could see the two huge drainage channels on either side that had been used to nearly empty Lake Powell. The side drainage channels sat empty in the morning sun. The main lower drainage port still discharged water, but the volume was tiny compared with the past.

In 2036, Lake Powell was only about 10 percent full, and just enough water flowed out of the dam to allow some creatures to continue living in the lower Colorado. Lake Mead, 326 miles below, had dropped to about 25 to 30 percent full, and electric production for Glen Canyon and Hoover Dams had ceased many years earlier because not enough water pressure remained to turn the giant turbines in either dam.

Yang now turned his gaze to the much-diminished Lake Powell. Recreational boaters had once sailed their houseboats out onto the water every summer and enjoyed weeks lying out on their decks, exploring the side canyons, and hiking the side trails. Now, northeast of the remaining water, there was nothing but empty lake bed and the large solar array field. A few dust devils blew in the far distance.

Yang remembered the days when he was a public information liaison in the visitor center, doling out figures on the dam and how much power it could generate. He used to take tours down into the bowels of the dam, where the giant turbines and magnets wrapped with wire generated 1,320 megawatts of power daily that was sent all over the Southwest. The turbines had long ceased to rotate and now were rusting into extinction. He used to take visitors across the top of the dam to gaze down the dam face, 710 feet to the Colorado River below. Tour boats below the dam would take visitors down the river for a three-hour excursion. That seemed like centuries ago.

He was thirsty already. He went back into his office and filled a water cup from a special spigot. The spigot connected to a fifty-gallon water tank that was filled monthly by a truck from Las Vegas. Since his new, deeper office had been constructed, the price of water had gone from eleven dollars a gallon to twenty-eight dollars a gallon. Clean drinking water was much harder to find. Vegas was one of only a few cities that had any well water left at all, and the wells there had to be drilled deeper every year. Even so, the city wells in Vegas were now beginning to reach brackish water. The large pipe that Vegas had sent deep into the bottom of Lake Mead in 2017 had to be extended farther into the lake because of evaporation. The thirty-foot-diameter pipe, known as "the straw," was getting plugged up with silt from the bottom of the lake, and as a result, Vegas was forced to invest millions of dollars into deeper wells, now reaching two thousand feet below the surface.

The sad thing was that most of the deep aquifers in Arizona, California, and Nevada were mostly tapped out. They had filled slowly for hundreds of thousands of years before early humans came over the ancient land bridge to North America, and very little remained of that ancient water. It would take another hundred thousand years to replenish, and at the present rate of use, it was unlikely the aquifers would ever be restored.

The larger cities such as Phoenix had seen their supply of Central Arizona Project canal water dwindle to a very small percentage of what used to flow. The Salt River Project reservoirs east of Phoenix—Roosevelt Lake and Saguaro Lake—had long since nearly dried out. As a result, a large amount of the municipal supplies was now trucked in from more water-rich states, such as Colorado and Nevada. A multitude of large tanker trucks, some larger than a railroad tank car, could be seen on the freeways daily. And water prices in the larger metropolitan areas had skyrocketed with the shortages. Most residents were now paying more for their monthly water than for their mortgages.

And speaking of mortgages, once word had gotten out about the water shortages, property and land prices in Arizona cities had plummeted. In 2019, Phoenix had boasted 4.6 million residents and was receiving an influx of over seventy-five thousand new residents yearly, mostly driven by drought and climate-caused fires in California. State leaders encouraged new business expansion and a continuing inflow of new residents, believing that the water would somehow take care of itself. Some even refused to believe that a drought existed.

Now in 2036, scientists weren't sure when the drought would end. They had warned that the Southwest had experienced several megadroughts since the year 1500, some for as long as fifty years or more. But again, optimism, capitalism, and denial of global warming had closed the minds of most state leaders. They were now backpedaling frantically and helplessly watching their state suffer a major water catastrophe.

Water was not the only scarce commodity. Food supplies were on the verge of becoming problematic too. Most of the dairy farms south of Phoenix had long since gone out of business. Only one or two major dairies were still in existence in Arizona. A combination of lack of alfalfa farms and water shortages had driven most out of the state. Lettuce and spinach farms, once filling the land around Yuma, were becoming scarce. A lot of food was being trucked in from other states, such as California, which of course had its own water and food problems. As a result, food prices were astronomical. Only the day before, when Yang had gone to the only grocery in Page, he had paid twenty dollars for a gallon of milk and twenty-five dollars for a pound of beef.

Yang now broke away from his ruminations and glanced again at his watch thermometer. It read 126 degrees. He jumped in his jeep and drove the four miles to another observing office above ground, north of the dam. Looking northeast, he could just make out the edge of the Grand Staircase-Escalante National Monument.

As Yang looked to the northeast, he squinted from the reflections coming off nearly 100,000 solar panels and another 175,000 solar reflectors that sent the sun's energy into pipes of liquid sodium and from there into an underground storage area. The First Solar Corporation in 2026 had arrived in Page and built the largest solar array field in the US in the northern section of the mostly drained lake basin. The field extended from the north end of the current small lake to where the old inflow river channels used to supply the larger lake. The field encompassed roughly 90 percent of the previous lake's size.

David Yang was reinvigorated and felt like fifty-five since taking the new job. He had taken a position with the First Solar Corporation as chief observer as soon as the solar array was built. The job required him only to monitor a computer that continuously scanned the array for energy output and the angles of the solar panels and the reflectors. If something seemed off, he would check the array area visually with his binoculars. Then all he had to do was to alert the maintenance team, and they would go into the lakebed and solve the problem.

The only problem with this arrangement was that the observer platform sat on top of the edge of the lake, up from the dam a bit, and the daytime temperatures in that area could reach 130 degrees Fahrenheit in summer. Therefore, Yang could only stay on the inside of the observing platform for fifteen minutes at a time since nothing could keep the inside cool for very long at that temperature.

He swept the lake area with powerful binoculars, searching for problems that he had seen earlier that day on the computer. A dark area in the middle of one solar array looked unusual. He checked the computer scan. Sure enough, the angle on that array was off by fifteen degrees, leading to a lack of sun reflection as seen from his office. He immediately called the operations team in Page and alerted them to the potential problem. In a few minutes they would be driving their jeeps down into the lake to fix it.

As Yang looked around the room of the observing platform, he saw an old announcement from the Coconino County Health Department: "Hantavirus outbreak."

The date was summer 2035, just last summer. Along with the water and food shortages, the climate had begun to favor certain organisms, Hantavirus among them. The virus had been found the previous summer in one of the maintenance team's quarters on the other side of the dam face, and three workers had died of the disease. Since then, Yang had been on the lookout for the pesky mice that harbored the virus. They occasionally made their homes in his quarters. But he had seen none this year and felt relieved.

While Yang was in the observing platform, his phone rang, and his wife Julia, was on the line. Her voice sounded unusually stressed.

"David, I'm having trouble filling this week's grocery list! I went to the Page market, and the owner told me that there were no shipments of lettuce or vegetables this week. And guess what. The milk shipments have stopped from Casa Grande Dairy south of Phoenix. Apparently, that dairy has also gone out of business. Now we're down to one large dairy left in the state. That means we may have to get our milk from Vegas or do without."

"Well, I'm not surprised. Since I took this job, I knew we would have to do without some things. I guess we'll just have to team up with one of the repair teams' families and place a combined order so it's delivered from Vegas or Flag. By the way, what's the news on Kristen's application for college at Northern Arizona University?"

"Well, she heard today that she couldn't be accepted this year. Something about a bunch of the professors leaving because of the drought. I guess she'll have to reapply to a community college in Vegas since Vegas seems to be the only major nearby city to have anything of a water supply left. But that's going to mean relocating there for the semester. It's a three hundred-mile drive."

David knew that his daughter had worked long and hard to get into NAU and had scored high on the college admission test. Now she would have to make other plans.

"Got to go, honey. The temperature in my observing office just hit 127 degrees. I've been here for twenty-five minutes already. See you for dinner."

Yang hung up the phone. From his upper observation office, he could see another one of the large water tanker trucks moving slowly across the new US 89. He looked behind the water tanker and could see a small line of cars headed across the new bridge.

"Damn fools," he said to himself. "It's going to hit 135 today, and the next water after Page isn't until Moab,

Mesa Verde, or Chaco! They'll be lucky to get even half a gallon in Page."

Now overheated, Yang headed back in his jeep to get to his cool underground office below the visitor center.

JULY 11

INTO PAGE

AIR TEMP 127°F, 12:00 P.M.

STONE IN THE SUPER PRIUS made his way from the bridge slowly up the canyon bank and on into Page. The water tanker that he had followed earlier had arrived in Page and discharged its load. Occasionally, when the water tankers stopped to unload, groups of locals with empty containers would run up to the driver and ask if he could spare a little water. Depending on the location, he might oblige, for a fee. In a few recent instances, though, armed bandits had begun to appear and had, in some cases, drained the entire contents of the tanker into their trucks. With the high price of water, they would then drive to another location, usually a town that hadn't had a delivery in a while, and sell the water for a profit. Two weeks ago, in Winslow, Arizona, a driver had been shot dead by such bandits.

Stone reached the top of the hill that led into Page. A few old signs advertised the only three motels left. As he drove farther, he stopped at a small shopping center and parked the Super Prius. A grocery, a restaurant, and a few tourist shops filled the square. He found a charging station to charge the car while he went into the restaurant for a late lunch. A young man approached him with a menu. Stone ordered a hamburger, some home-made bread, and an electrolyte drink. When the waiter returned with the food, he apologized.

"Sorry about the beef. We only get a beef shipment now once every two weeks from Vegas, that's usually frozen, and it may not taste too good."

Stone took a few bites of the burger but then stopped.

"You're right. It tastes like cardboard. I think I'll just finish the bread. Oh, I'd like some more electrolyte soda to go. I'm heading down to Horseshoe Bend to take some photos, and I know it's going to be hot."

"You can say that again. It hit 130 yesterday and stuck above 128 all last week. When I'm not working here, I double for the solar array repair crew. But even then, when I'm out on the lake bed during the day, I have to wear special protective cooling clothing that reflects the sun's light. That includes cooling vests. We had a repair-man faint out there last week when it hit 130. You have to bring along extra electrolyte drinks. By the way, watch out for tourists at the Bend. We're one of the stops on the Southwest bus tours. They seem to get about seventy of them on one bus. So many that the rangers had to put a two-bus, one-hour limit on the parking there. But I'm glad they come to Page. Keeps the restaurant open."

Stone gave the waiter $55.80 for the hamburger, bread, and drinks and headed out the door. The sun felt intense on the top of his head, and he quickly put his hiking hat on.

As he pulled out of the shopping center, he saw a sign for one of the motels:

"Best Motel in Page—$250/Night—Free Breakfast."

Stone registered and went directly to his room. He was tired from the drive and the sun and settled in for a nap since it was too early in the day for good photos at the Bend. He took the briefcase and travel pack inside and laid them on a table in the room. He forgot to set an alarm and woke up at 4:00 p.m. to the noise of a loud motorcycle outside. Realizing that he had overslept, he quickly grabbed the travel pack containing his camera gear and headed outside.

JULY 11

HORSESHOE BEND
NEAR PAGE

AIR TEMP 130°F, 4:00 P.M.

STONE HEADED WEST and then south on 89. A sign on the right announced, "Horseshoe Bend Tourist Area One Mile Ahead. Two-Bus Limit for One Hour—Car Limit 25. Entrance fee $200. Caution—Traffic Approaching from the South."

As he turned into the Horseshoe Bend area, he saw two large tourist buses with travel logos on the side that were parked at the farthest end of the parking area.

About a dozen cars filled the remaining spots. He waited as one car pulled out and then quickly parked the Super Prius. Tourists could be seen moving to and fro like small ants along the path toward the overlook. Stone noticed some unusual rock formations in the distance that reminded him of The Wave. He glanced at the outside thermometer on the car—130 degrees at 4:30 p.m. Another thermometer on the path outside for tourists read 129.5.

This has to be a quick trip, he thought. Then he noticed a vendor in an RV renting cooling vests. He decided to get one so he could stay out a little longer and get the perfect shot. He grabbed his travel pack, extra electrolyte drinks, his hiking hat, and the vest, and he headed down the trail. He left the AC on in the car to stay at 78 degrees internal.

It was about 1/3 mile to the edge of the viewing area, and he could see the large fence ahead. As the ranger had told him, it had been installed to protect tourists and keep them from falling to their deaths over the one thousand-foot cliff. The fence stretched from his leftmost vision all the way to the right. It appeared to be about 1/4 mile long and about four feet tall. Several groups of people had parked themselves behind it and were gaping at the vista beyond, some taking photos. As Stone came closer, he could see that he was going to have a difficult time finding a clear shot of the scenery.

He moved off the path and headed to the right, where he could just see the edge of the fence in the distance. The ground here was hard and pitted, with several colors of yellow and gray. Some layers stood out in the distance, reminding him again of The Wave. As he moved toward the fence edge, the ground became difficult to walk on, and he had a little trouble carrying the weight of his camera gear.

He picked out an area a bit away from the right side of the fence and approached the cliff edge there cautiously. A sign on the edge of the fence read, "DANGER! EXTREME CAUTION ADVISED! High Risk Area for Accidental Falls. Do Not Go Beyond Fence. Stand Here at Your Own Risk. 1,000-foot Drop."

Undeterred, Stone grabbed his travel pack, unpacked his photo equipment, and began to set up a small tripod near the cliff edge for a wide-angle shot. The sun's angle wasn't quite right now, but he was prepared to wait a little longer for a better shot when the sun started to go down behind the cliffs.

The sounds of nearby conversation broke his concentration. Two young tourists were trying to take a selfie with a phone so thin it reflected off the sun like a mirror. They couldn't be over twenty. The girl's voice giggled in the wind. Stone heard her say, "No . . . closer . . . let's get a better shot."

They seemed to be moving slowly toward the edge of the cliff face, ignoring the sign on the fence. The woman's face was pointed back at her partner as she tried to maneuver her phone. They were both totally preoccupied in the moment.

Stone shook his head—always someone taking selfies!—put his travel pack down near the edge, and put a rock on top of it. He went back to setting up the exposure.

He spent a minute fixing the exposure exactly with one of the new filters he had brought.

It was a splendid view. One could see the thin green Colorado below, curling in a clockwise direction around a large bluff on the other side, which looked to be about nine hundred feet high. The bluff had several layers of rock embedded in it. In ancient times, Native Americans had used a footpath to cross the river below. The river would have been much wider back then. The old ones would have climbed down the near side, crossed the river at about a six- to seven-foot depth, and then climbed the nine hundred feet to the top on the other side. It would have been quite arduous. The trail would have taken them deep onto the plateau, extending for many miles west of Page. They would have used the trail to hunt and for lookout positions on the other side.

The click of Stone's shutter sounded just as a loud scream broke off to his left side.

"Taylor, you're too close!"

Stone glanced to the left and was horrified. He saw the girl with the phone, who had moved closer to him than he had realized, lose her footing and plunge over the edge, taking his travel pack along with her. She had dislodged it with her foot.

A long scream started and seemed to go on forever. It lasted for about eight to nine seconds. It went quickly from higher to lower pitch, like a train receding. As Stone watched, time seemed to dilate—and he noticed every detail of the girl falling: the color of her dress, her black hair, her hands flailing wildly, her body rotating slowly, the pure blue color of the sky—the girl's companion screaming. Then it all suddenly stopped, with a small *thud* from below as she hit the river's edge.

He looked farther over the edge to see the terrible sight of the girl lying on some rocks near the river, her red blood beginning to spill into the green water. It didn't seem real. But with his medical training, he knew immediately, based on the height of the fall, that there was probably no chance she was still alive.

"Oh my God. Oh my God. Taylor!" her boyfriend screamed over and over. "Help! Please help! Help me!" he cried as he turned to Stone. He stood gaping over the edge at the scene below.

"Come on. Let's try to get the ranger!" Stone shouted.

The young man looked panic-stricken and just stood there frozen to the spot, still calling his girlfriend's name. Unable to move him, Stone ran back toward the asphalt path to get help. Others heard the screams and began to run over to their location. Stone's tripod still stood near the edge, but in the moment, he left everything behind, including his camera.

After running about 1/8 of a mile, he spied a ranger on the path and cried,

"Help. We need help! Someone's gone over the cliff! Do you have a rescue team?"

The ranger quickly came over to him, and Stone

explained what had happened. The ranger also knew from experience what the likely outcome would be.

"We have a helo rescue available at the Page airport—I'll call them!"

While Stone stood there, he heard the ranger say, "Helo One, we need a rescue chopper ASAP. Girl went over the edge down in the Bend Canyon—urgency level one!"

"Roger that. Leaving immediately. ETA four minutes," came the response.

At the Page airport, the pilot put down his coffee and ran to his chopper. He had functioned as pilot and EMT ever since rescue funding had been cut when Page had lost most of its population. Some money still came in because hikers and paleontologists in the Grand Staircase-Escalante needed rescue occasionally, and the solar array repair crew needed transport when they had to go farther up the lake bed.

The helicopter had some difficulty gaining traction in the thin, hot air, but eventually it headed for Horseshoe Bend. Stone and the ranger heard the high pitch of the chopper's approach and watched it set down on a hard area near the asphalt footpath. Tourists scattered left and right. Particles of yellow-brown 200 million-year-old dust from the Navajo Sandstone formation blew everywhere.

"Where?" yelled the pilot over the chopper sound.

"Over there, by the edge of the fence." Stone pointed to the last place he had seen the girl only minutes ago.

"I'd like to go along," Stone added over the noise of

the blades. "I'm a doctor. I can help. Also, my pack fell off with her. I need to find it."

The pilot pondered, "Well, normally, no . . . but . . . if you're willing to risk it, OK." He thought to himself it would be good to have another medical person onboard.

Stone climbed aboard and the chopper headed down over the edge where he had seen the girl fall. As they descended into the canyon opening, Stone could see the girl's boyfriend still frozen in horror on the edge above. As they came near the river, they both could see the out-stretched girl with her head contorted into an awkward position to one side. A moderate rivulet of blood flowed from one of her temples.

She lay near a large rock that had sharp points, and she had apparently fallen directly onto it. As they set-tled onto the riverbank, Stone tried to see where his pack might have fallen. He spied a piece of the pack, torn apart and dangling on another nearby rock. As he looked downstream, he could see a small orange and green object drifting slowly away from them—the rest of his pack and something else that he couldn't make out. It looked as though the pack had broken apart on the rock, just as the girl's head had broken. He turned his attention back to the girl.

The pilot and Stone stepped quickly out of the chop-per. The pilot placed his finger on the girl's carotid. There was no pulse, and when he put his hand on her head, the skull bones moved to one side with a perceptible "crunch." Stone looked down and was nauseated to see some brain material oozing from the crack in her skull.

Drawing upon his medical training, Stone pulled up both eyelids and saw that one pupil was visibly dilated.

"I think she probably died immediately," said the pilot.

"Yeah, I agree," Stone said reluctantly after closing the girl's eyes with his fingers.

They loaded the girl's body onto one side of the chopper and began to secure her.

"Really a shame, she's about the sixth fatality here in two years. I thought we had solved this with the fence, but I guess not, human nature being what it is."

"We were just beyond the fence," Stone offered.

"Well, then, you knew the risks," the pilot replied.

As the pilot finished securing the girl, Stone remembered his travel pack.

"I need a few minutes to go get my pack."

"Yeah, OK. She's not going anywhere."

As he started running quickly downstream toward the floating piece of pack, Stone could just make out the small orange-colored object floating on the surface in the middle of the river. It was rapidly distancing itself. He suddenly realized, Holy shit. It's the nanobot container! I must have left the bot cooler in the travel pack instead of in the room. Crap! That meant he had only half of the experimental bots left that he had brought from San Diego. And the bots he was staring at floating down the river were probably worth north of $6 million.

Stone ran quickly down the edge of the riverbank after the floating bot cooler, but by now it had gone some three hundred yards. He made a desperate attempt to reach the cooler, jumping into the warm water and trying to swim to it. But the current had picked up, and it was disappearing rapidly around the bend, along with what remained of the pack. Stone was not a strong swimmer and had to turn back, exhausted. As he waded onshore, his face turned red with anger at the loss of $6 million dollars floating just out of reach. All that work, he thought. He walked back to the chopper and tried to compose himself. After all, he did have another group of bots in his briefcase back at the motel. His anger turned slowly to resignation as he thought to himself, Thank God we decided to split the supply—half in the pack and half in the briefcase. I told Sorensen that was the right thing to do! I can't waste any more time, I need to get to Denver. I've got more than enough.

As Stone arrived back to the chopper, the blades began to turn slowly. Once Stone was seated inside, the pilot said, "I'll drop you up top where I got you and then take her body to the morgue. I'll tell the ranger and the boyfriend where he can find her."

As the chopper arrived back up at the top of the canyon, Stone noticed that the boyfriend had come up the path and was waiting for them, his face still contorted with sadness. After the blade noise died a bit, he ran up to the side of the chopper.

"Is there any hope? How is she?"

Then he noticed his girlfriend, or what was left of her, strapped to the other side of the helicopter. He began to call her name again and wail with loud sobs as he ran to her side. One glance at her head and he knew. Blood was still oozing there. Part of her scalp was missing from the fall.

The pilot turned to him and over the still whirring blades yelled, "I'm sorry, man. I believe she died instantly."

The young man laid his head on her lap and continued to cry.

The pilot continued, "I'm sorry. We have to go, but you can find her in the town hospital morgue near the eastern edge of town. Plug it into your GPS or ask anyone for directions."

Stone climbed out and thanked the pilot. Then, as the chopper took off, he saw the tourists scattering and the boyfriend sobbing, walking slowly and dejectedly back up the path toward his car.

Stone ran down the path to the place where his tripod and camera still stood. A large crowd had gathered and was staring first over the edge and then back up to where the helo ascended into the late afternoon air. Some people were still actually taking selfies.

Stone was disgusted. He grabbed his gear and walked back to his car, still ruminating about the girl and his lost nanobots.

As he tried to push the button for his door opener, he felt an intense pain and screamed, "Jesus, what the hell?"

The Super Prius had cool-door regulators, but he must have forgotten to activate them upon leaving the car. Now the tip of his forefinger throbbed and grew increasingly pink. Slowly a large blister developed where he had touched the car surface.

"Holy shit. Damn. Now I've got to get *this* taken care of. What a fucking waste of an afternoon." He turned on the car and asked Io: "Urgent care. Page." The voice came back: "Page. Urgent Care. Two miles up Main Street."

As he drove back into town, he saw the sign: "Urgent Care—Only One for 200 miles. Seven to Seven. Cash Only."

He went inside the clinic. There was a registrar and one provider in a white coat, but except for them, it was empty. A tall, thin, attractive woman, who couldn't be more than twenty-five, quickly put him in a treatment room.

"What happened to you? You one of those solar repair men?" she said as she examined his finger.

"Nope, just burned it on my car door."

"Well, won't be the first time. Let me see it."

He felt the familiar rise in his groin but couldn't acknowledge it. He was in too much pain.

The young PA quickly sterilized the blister with Betadine, then popped it with a scalpel. After giving Stone a tetanus shot, she said, "You'll feel better now."

She placed some Silvadene antibiotic cream over it,

then a nonstick dressing, and then she wrapped it with a piece of gauze.

"Leave this on for at least a day, and then open it to the air. You shouldn't have any problem."

As Stone was paying his bill, the clinic door opened, and an older man with a First Solar logo on his outer heat suit appeared with one of his companions. His companion looked concerned and said, "He passed out twenty minutes ago out on the solar field, and we couldn't get him back right away. Please take a look."

"OK, bring him into the exam room," replied the PA as she yelled for the receptionist to bring the life support equipment and an IV into the room.

Stone drove back down the street to get some supplies at the shopping center he had been in earlier that day. He bought six gallons of electrolyte solution, some carbs for snacks, and emergency supplies—food, water, batteries, extra hats. It might be another two or three days before he hit a population center of any consequence, and he had already seen what might happen if the Prius malfunctioned.

Now, as he left the store, a vague tiredness set in. His energy felt used up.

No wonder, with the event near the Bend, the helicopter ride, and the revelation that he had just lost $6 million worth of bots floating down the river.

It was nearly 7:30 p.m. by the time he left the store, so he decided to stay over for the night and plan the path forward on his trip. He drove back to the motel where he had napped, and he double-checked that the other bot pack was still in the briefcase. He took it out and set it on the table.

He pulled a frozen dinner from the supplies he had purchased, heated it up in the microwave, and ate slowly, still digesting what had happened at the Bend. Stone consulted a travel map on his phone for the next day's journey and was then quickly asleep.

JULY 12

ON THE
NAVAJO NATION

AIR TEMP 111°F, 7:30 A.M.

THE NEXT MORNING, Stone woke up refreshed. Yesterday had been a trying day. But he was eager to get on the road to Denver. The phase III trial would be starting in a few days, and he wanted to get there as soon as possible. The fact that he had lost half of his bot samples still disturbed him. Sorensen would be upset back in San Diego, but Stone's ego and experience told him that he could get more bots made quickly in his factory if he needed them. His investors were eager for a return. He had spent many hours in meetings recruiting them, and they would certainly be happy to give him more money.

The Super Prius headed east on Arizona 98 toward Black Mesa and the turnoff for US 160. It was 7:30 a.m., and the outside temp read 111°. He voice-activated the system that controlled the engine cooling and set it for moderate. He didn't want a repeat of the problem he'd had coming into Page. His route would take him across many miles of empty plateau, where only a few hardy Navajo lived. Their springs and well water supplies had dried up long ago, and their only source now was the tanker trucks. But even so, the truckers often had to be bribed, and if they had unloaded all their water in the last town, it could be two weeks between deliveries.

As Stone approached US 160, he could see Black Mesa in the distance and Navajo Mountain looming in the distance off his left shoulder. In years past, the mesa was the main source of coal for the Navajo Generating Station east of Page. Three diesel trains a day would make the forty-five-mile trip to Page, where the coal was stored in large piles next to the plant. But in 2019, no new buyer could be found for the coal-fired plant, and it was decommissioned. It was now a relic crumbling in the heat.

Heading north on US 160, Stone saw mirages that looked like small lakes in the distance. He drove into Kayenta, near Monument Valley. Kayenta, like a lot of the tourist attractions in northern Arizona, had shrunk and now boasted only a few motels. He saw a few tourist buses, mostly from out of state. A sign read, "Water $29/Gallon."

Stone was glad he had bought extra water in Page, where it had been cheaper. He then glanced at his electric charge gauge. It read 94 percent. Good enough!

A half hour later, he passed Teec Nos Pos and crossed into New Mexico. He saw a few hogans in the distance, baking in the heat. The unusual formation of Shiprock appeared in another twenty minutes. Stone stopped by the side of the road briefly to photograph the formation. At the town of Shiprock, he headed south on US 491 so that he could pick up Interstate 40 at Gallup and then head east through New Mexico and on into Colorado. About 1:00 p.m. he stopped in Gallup, elevation 6,512 feet. He noted it was only twenty-five miles from there to Window Rock, the site of the Navajo Nation tribal headquarters, but he decided not to take the side trip.

He pulled into a restaurant in Gallup and walked inside. Several Navajo sat around tables. They looked surprised as he sat down since few tourists stopped in Gallup at that point. The outside temperature read 125 degrees on the thermometer seen through the window. He ordered a hamburger, fries, and a tall electrolyte solution from the kiosk. An older native came over to deliver his order.

"Where you headed?" he asked.

"I'm going on to Albuquerque, Santa Fe, and then Denver."

"Have you heard the forecast?"

"Which one?" Stone replied.

"Well, there's a huge high coming in from LA, covering most of northern Arizona, and then tracking on through northern New Mexico, even into southern

Colorado. They're talking about 130 degrees possibly here by the weekend."

Stone shrugged.

"Yeah, I heard that a couple days ago in Page, but I appreciate you letting me know." After finishing his meal, Stone approached the man and said, "I think I'll get four or five extra electrolyte quarts to go."

"Sure. Sounds like a good plan. You'll need it."

As Stone headed outside to the Prius, he felt well supplied with fluids.

He avoided touching the door button with his bandaged hand, got in, reset the AC temperature to keep himself and the bots cool, and headed out onto Interstate 40. Santa Fe lay two hours ahead if he drove straight through. Then by late evening he'd reach Denver, where the researchers were waiting.

Albuquerque was an hour and a half drive to the east. The Super Prius purred along at 115 mph, and Jeremy was happy to put the car on autopilot so he could take in the sights. After about forty minutes, off to the left he spied Mount Taylor, one of the four sacred mountains of the Navajo. His route took him through two small mountain ranges, and as he picked them out, he noticed that the normally green covering of pinyon pine and evergreens had been reduced markedly. Only a few scraggly brown trees covered the base of the mountains. Fire warning signs were everywhere. In the distance he thought he could see a smoke pillar, which was surely a forest fire. The number of forest fires, particularly in New Mexico and Arizona, had risen to record numbers, and the states were having difficulty keeping up with them.

As he approached Albuquerque, he noticed an ominous sign: "WARNING! WATER BANDITS! Keep Your Car Locked. Only Stop at State Rest Areas."

And then another sign: "Water $35/Gallon. Limited Supply. Use Only State-Controlled Water Access."

Stone pondered the meaning of both signs. Water bandits were obvious, but he had no idea what "state-controlled water access" meant.

It was the middle of the afternoon. He called up the outside temp. The onboard computer replied, "128 and rising."

Albuquerque, like a lot of southwestern cities, had lost much of its population due to decreasing water supplies and elevated temperatures. Once boasting 1.5 million residents, it now held only 250,000. The Rio Grande River, which ran right through the city, had long been stressed by population growth and overfarming. Like the Colorado River in Arizona, the Rio Grande had become a vestige of what it once was. As a result, Albuquerque had to dig deep for water.

Back in the early 2020s, the city's wells were at a depth of 350 feet. Now, in 2036, Jeremy could see multiple tall well towers surrounding the edge of the city. Many had reached depths of twenty-three hundred feet. Unlike the coastal cities of California, Albuquerque had no ocean to process seawater, so it had to rely almost totally on its wells. The Rio Grande stopped flowing before reaching the southern border of New Mexico.

Stone pulled the Super Prius over at the junction of the 40 and the 25. He spied a drive-in and parked the car under the drive-in's sunshade. Before he could turn off the ignition, a man suddenly appeared at his driver's window. Stone quickly checked the lock, remembering the sign about bandits.

"You got water? Water?" the old man cried. He appeared to be about seventy, but it was hard to tell. He had a large, torn brimmed hat for sun protection, but his face was virtually blackened from the sun. His clothes were ripped and sported many holes. He looked terrible. Barely alive. Jeremy looked for a weapon on the man, but he didn't see one. Maybe the man was homeless.

He stared at the man and yelled through the window,

"No! *No water!*" Even though he felt some compassion for the man, he couldn't afford to give any of his supply away.

Suddenly, a waiter on magnetic skates appeared in front of the car and began to yell at the homeless man, "Hey! Get away from here. . . . Go. . . . Get out of here. *Now!*"

The man turned toward the waiter and, with a loud cry, repeated his demand,

"Water, water . . . need water . . . please . . . please . . ."

"No, no water. Now get out!"

Stone could see the waiter start to beat the man with a

hard stick, and after he knocked him down, the man ran away, crying, "Bastards, bastards." His voice trailed off.

"Sorry about that," the waiter said. "We get a lot of these homeless guys now. I don't know how they survive. I guess in the shelter downtown. But they can be annoying."

"There was a sign about water bandits coming into Albuquerque. What's the situation here?"

"Oh, yeah. You have to watch out. Ever since the Rio Grande dried up, we have a group of these people trying to steal water. With the price of water so high, they steal what they can and then try to resell it. You may see some of them when you leave the city. They usually try to stop tourists. But watch out. Some of them are armed."

"Wow. OK, thanks for the warning. Just bring me some electrolyte-agave drink. And I need four extra quarts. I'm on my way to Denver by way of Santa Fe."

"OK, coming right up."

The waiter fetched the drinks, and Jeremy paid and headed back on the road.

Sure enough, as he headed out of town, near Bernalillo, a suburb of Albuquerque, some men appeared at the side of the road and motioned him to pull over. They appeared to have assault rifles and were dressed in old clothing. But having been warned, Jeremy ordered the Super Prius to accelerate and blew out of range. A few shots ricocheted off his bumper as he headed north to Santa Fe.

Around Santa Fe, Jeremy again noticed some of the climate destruction and deforestation at this high elevation. After the temperatures had started to rise here, the pine beetle had come in to attack the evergreens. With the decreased water flow in the evergreen's roots and trunk, the beetle could get inside the bark, eventually killing the tree. Millions of acres had been decimated.

Jeremy made Raton Pass at the New Mexico-Colorado border by 5:00 p.m. and headed north toward Colorado Springs and Denver. As he went through the pass, at seventy-eight hundred feet in elevation, he called up the outside temperature. Even at this elevation, Io's voice said, "One hundred and twelve degrees."

He checked the AC system. No warnings. When he reached Pueblo at 6:00 p.m., he stopped for dinner. It had been a long day of driving, and he needed a brief rest.

He ordered some dinner at a roadside diner and then asked the waiter for some extra electrolyte solution. Even though Stone had been drinking the entire trip, his body had become slightly dehydrated, given the outside temperatures. And now he noticed a bit of fogginess in his thoughts along with the tiredness.

After dinner and the extra drinks, he felt refreshed as he climbed back into the Super Prius and headed north. The sun was setting over the Rockies as he passed through Colorado Springs. Beams of orange and purple light scattered off the car. An unusual sign appeared on the outskirts as he was leaving Colorado Springs:

"Denver 70 Miles. Cheapest Water in the West. Water: $12/Gallon."

Jeremy puzzled over the sign. After seeing water prices climb to twenty-seven dollars per gallon and more in Arizona and New Mexico, this seemed like an anomaly.

But Denver had been wiser than most other cities when climate change hit. In 2019, Colorado had agreed to the Drought Contingency Plan with the other six Colorado River watershed states. The plan was designed to help keep more water in the Lake Mead reservoir by calling for minor cutbacks to some of the farmers and cities in the member states. At the time, Denver was working on a new water pipeline to transport water over the Rocky Mountains into the city. And the Drought Contingency Plan was just what Denver and the state of Colorado needed to motivate them to finish it quickly.

When the DCP was signed, Denver relied on several mountain reservoirs and wells. But the wells were starting to tap out and had to be dug much deeper. Some of the wells reached the two-thousand-foot level. The Ogallala Aquifer, a huge aquifer covering five midwestern states and Colorado, was rapidly being drained due to overallocation, intensive farming, and ranching.

Denver's new pipeline made up for the declining well water and ground water so that Denver, unlike many other western cities in 2036, had a relatively sustainable supply.

It was dark when the Super Prius reached Denver. Stone texted Dr. Marc Casper, the head of research at Banner Denver West and Stone's friend, that he had finally arrived in Denver. The two friends planned to meet the next morning in Casper's office at the large teaching and research hospital where the trial would take place.

JULY 13

OFFICE OF MARC CASPER, PHD

AIR TEMP 105°F, 8:00 A.M.

"MARC, GREAT TO SEE you again!"

"Likewise, Jeremy. How was your trip?"

"Long."

"I'm sure."

"Yeah, you know I'm a photo buff. Got a new wide-angle lens last month, and so I stopped along the way to take some pictures." Stone showed Casper the photos over a cup of coffee. He soon came to the shots around Horseshoe Bend.

"Marc, you won't believe this. When I was photographing Horseshoe Bend, I was taking some incredible pics when this stupid young woman taking a selfie backed into my area and fell over the edge! It was terrifying. She was killed, of course, and when she fell, she knocked my travel pack over with her. The pack broke apart and floated down the Colorado. Unfortunately, half the bots were in the pack! I forgot to take them out of the pack when I rested at a motel in Page."

Casper looked horrified. Stone continued, "So those bots all went down the river at Horseshoe, some 192 billion of them."

"What!? Are you kidding me? Do we have enough for the trial?"

"Fortunately, yes. Before I left San Diego, Sorensen and I calculated that the remaining 192 billion would be more than enough. That was the reason for separating them into two groups, in case one of the coolers failed during the trip or something else happened."

"Well, good. I'm relieved. And I'm glad you arrived last night. The patients for the trial are all here, ready to go. My research staff is eager to get started.

"The control groups have been carefully matched to the treatment group by age, type of cancer, smoking history, blood pressure, cholesterol level, kidney function. And one of the control groups is cancer-free. That group will be treated with some of the nanobots to look closely again for any adverse effects. They've all signed releases, and the NIH paperwork has been completed. And they've all been counseled regarding the risks of the trial."

"Sounds like everything's in order. Thanks again, Marc, for allowing me to do the trial here. As you know, a lot of places, even some of the best hospitals and centers in California, weren't willing to take a risk on my new nanomachine. After that death in San Francisco last year in that clinical trial of another group's nanobot, everyone freaked out. And anyway, in my opinion, your research center is one of the world's best."

"Well, we've been friends for a long time now, way back to the postdoc days. Besides, I've looked at your animal experiments and the Phase I and II trial data in detail, and I really think this could be a breakthrough for patients if it works."

"Yes, I think so too."

At that moment, a woman in her late 30s came into the room.

"Jeremy, this is Dr. Joanna Hsu, my research assistant."

"Good to meet you," Jeremy said, even as he noticed her well-endowed breasts. "So, you'll be helping Marc on this?"

"Yes, we're looking forward to working with you. I've spent my whole career working on lung cancer treatment, and like Marc says, we're hopeful that this new treatment will revolutionize cancer therapy. Of course, Marc and I have read all the experimental research on your bot up until now. It's quite impressive. Are there any specific issues we need to know about regarding the nanomachines?"

"Well, they've been traveling with me in special

coolers while I had them in the car, so I'll have to show you how to remove them. Also, they're in a special nonmagnetic fluid. And you'll have to keep their temperatures low until you inject them into the patients."

"OK, let's get started," she said.

Stone opened his briefcase, checked the temperature control on the bot cooler, and handed the cooler over to the two researchers.

"Oh, one more thing. Just be sure you're gloved when handling that liquid.

"And you may want to remove them in a hood. The liquid can be somewhat irritating. After you take them out of the cooler, place them into a cool solution of normal saline for the injection, and warm them slowly to 5 degrees below body temperature. The patient's body will then take over. Also, be careful how you handle them when you are diluting the dosages."

"OK, thanks for the advice."

With that, Stone followed Casper and Hsu into another room, where they transferred the bots into cooled saline. Several researchers were standing in the area, waiting for the trial to begin.

"I'd like to inject the first patient, if that's OK," Stone said.

"Of course. It's your trial."

After the syringes were readied, Stone steadied himself and injected the first patient. The patient was a forty-seven-year-old man who had already been through radiation, lung surgery, and chemotherapy for his disease. He looked thin, and his skin had a pasty coloration from all the treatments. But as Stone brought his hand close to the inside of his elbow for the injection, the man looked up at Stone and said, "Dr. Stone, I know I volunteered for this trial, and there's no guarantee, but I wanted to thank you for your effort in developing this treatment."

Stone, though fairly egotistical, still maintained some human empathy. He looked directly into the patient's eyes and said, "We're really quite hopeful about this treatment. All of the animal and human data so far tell us that we're going to be successful."

The man smiled as Stone finished the injection. Stone then went down to the cafeteria for some coffee. He planned to stay in Denver for most of the trial in case he was needed, particularly if something went wrong. It had been a long process designing, producing, and testing the nanomachine, and he couldn't wait to see if all the hours would pay off.

Both Stone and Sorensen stood to profit immensely if the nanobot succeeded even modestly in treating lung cancer in humans. They were ready to go with a final patent for the machine should the Denver trial succeed. Money had already been raised for further production from Stone's funders. Many of the funders were other scientists interested in Stone's work.

The next morning, Stone visited the research center at Banner West.

Several research assistants in white coats were busy monitoring the subjects, taking their vital signs regularly, and drawing labs, checking for side effects. Each carried a small notepad into which the data on the patients was dictated. The trial was designed to take three to four months, and Stone was eager to see if his nanomachine could change the course of the cancers in the trial patients.

JULY 12

LEES FERRY, ARIZONA, ON THE COLORADO RIVER

AIR TEMP 125°F, 11:00 A.M.

"SHIT, IT'S HOT, HONEY," Tyler called out.

"I know, just be patient. We'll get some drinks in Page in a little while."

"It's 125 in the shade!"

"I know. It's really heating up. "

Tyler went to the water's edge, grabbed a handful of river water, drank quickly, and headed back to the van.

"Come on, honey. Let's get going."

"OK, I'm ready. Hit the AC!"

The van pulled out of the area where Tyler and his wife, Jenna, had been kayaking and headed down Alt 89, then up 89 toward Page.

It took them about an hour to get into town, the van's

engine cranking in the heat. Mirages of striated hills loomed in the distance.

"Boy, that water tasted mighty junky!"

"What? Did you actually drink that river water?" Jenna asked. "Are you nuts? That water's probably got everything in it from sheep dung to parasites!"

"Maybe, but I couldn't wait. The kayaking burned me up, even though we were only on the river about thirty-five minutes. Nah, it's so warm anyway, probably killed all that stuff off. Besides, I was dying of thirst."

They ate lunch at a small restaurant in Page, then headed back to their motel for a long nap. The kayaking and heat had indeed worn them out. They went back to the restaurant in the early evening. Tyler ordered a rare hamburger, fries, and some electrolyte soda. Jenna settled for cold veggie soup and an ice cream stick.

"Mmm, this tastes really good," she said, "Cold food in this heat is a luxury."

"Yeah," he said, then coughed slightly. "Feels like I've got some dust in my throat."

"I know. It's everywhere. I heard from the guide that they even have tall dust walls, or dust barriers around the lake bed to protect the solar arrays. There's so much dust on the wind."

After Tyler took another bite of the burger, he noticed a slightly pinkish stain on his napkin where it touched the corner of his mouth.

"Huh, must be the rare burger."

After dinner, the two headed back down the 17 to Phoenix. It was much cooler to travel at night.

ON THE NAVAJO NATION

AIR TEMP 130°F, 5:00 P.M.

ADAM MANY GOATS stepped out of his hogan in the late afternoon. The sun was lying low in the west as he felt the afternoon's heat hit his forehead. Adam had been alone for four years, ever since his wife had died of cancer and his two grown sons moved away to Utah three years before.

It was the time of the year when the Navajo were grazing their sheep herds on what remained of the summer grasses on the plateau. Adam was eager to round up his sheep for the night and bring them up to the pen, where he kept them near his house.

Seems awfully warm, he thought as he called for his horse, Maikoh. His horse had been with him for many years, and as he put on the saddle blanket, he could see the gray hairs that now crowded the horse's mane.

Maikoh stood perfectly still as Adam finished with the blanket and gave him some hay. As he brushed the mane, Adam noticed something unusual.

Several huge greenish-brown grasshoppers about three inches long were latched onto Maikoh's mane. As he looked over the rest of the thin horse, he noticed a bunch more climbing up the horse's rear and legs. It was the middle of summer, and the insects could normally be seen only in the late fall, when the Navajo harvested their crops: corn, squash, beans, and wheat. In fact, the insects had caused more damage to the crops recently as the temperatures had risen on the plateau. They were beginning to decimate some of the local fields. Adam started to lead the horse down the plateau, feeling the crunch of hoppers under his feet.

As he looked down the plateau, he could see that the grasshoppers lay all over the ground and were busy working at whatever weeds and grass they could find.

Adam owned about twenty sheep, which he sold for meat or sheared for wool. Most of the sheep were older now, but he had a few younger sheep for breeding. The younger ones had been a gift from his clan cousin. They would usually feed on the slim grasses and weeds that grew on the plateau near his house. However, lately, with the rising temperatures, little grass could be found. He sometimes had to borrow hay or fodder from his relatives to make it through the summer, and several of the sheep had died recently, mostly from malnutrition or lack of water.

Water was a major problem for Adam, and in fact, for many Navajo now.

In the last several years, Adam had watched helplessly as the rainfall on his upper plateau had dwindled to almost nothing, punctuated by the extremely rare thunderstorms in the late summer. The watering hole near his house was desiccated. As a result, he had to take his herd farther and farther away just to find water. More often now, too, he would have to bribe the water trucks just to keep the herd alive.

Adam spied the herd in the distance down the slope of the plateau. They appeared to be in a large group down near the bank of the river.

The Colorado, or what was left of it after the Glen Canyon dam had nearly been drained, wandered slowly in a southerly direction on the edge of his property and the property of his clan. This was where he found most of his sheep today, standing up to their knees in the greenish water. Their loud bleating was a welcome sound.

As he brought his horse to a stop and tied the horse to a large rock, Adam could see the result of the recent temperature climb on the herd. Instead of thick wool, most of them now had only a scraggly orangish-brown coat, and even then the wool was hanging loosely on only a few body parts.

He could remember when the summer temperatures in this region had never risen beyond 105 or 107. That was years ago. Now, on summer days like today, 128 and even 130 had been recorded. That was why the sheep usually spent much of their time either near or in the river. It was the coolest place around.

As he dismounted Maikoh, more large hoppers crunched under his feet. Several alighted on his shoulders and began chewing on his shirt. There were so many that it began to bother him. He also noticed that a lot of the sheep were covered with the insects. They appeared irritated by the pests, and some were clearly annoyed with the frustration of not being able to get rid of them.

It looked to Adam that all the sheep were here together in the river. As he scanned the herd, he noticed one of his older sheep off to the right lying on its side at the river's edge. Its wool was almost completely gone, a result of lack of water and the brutally high temperatures. As Adam approached the animal, it started to gaze up at him, but then its head fell back down again on the riverbank.

Its eyes were listless as it lay there. He could see the outline of the animal's thin ribs rise and fall in a somewhat rapid succession. He was concerned, since his herd had recently fallen below twenty and now one more animal appeared to be sick.

He bent down to examine the sheep and saw something that startled him. A slow drip of brownish blood oozed from the sheep's behind. A little pool of the blood could be seen blending with the greenish water in the late afternoon light. The animal lay motionless, unaware of Adam's closeness.

Adam began to puzzle about this. He examined the sheep's body for cuts or scratches or signs that the animal had been injured. It wasn't unusual for the sheep to be attacked by wild dogs in the area, but Adam found no bite marks or other injuries. As he looked closer and went through the hide, he noticed no fang marks that could be explained by a nearby rattler—no bullet holes that could have been made by local poachers.

Ya' ad' dila,' Adam thought and then said aloud, "Why is this happening to me?" For Adam, this discovery broke the Navajo law of Hozho, or beauty in the world. The Navajo believed that beauty is above, below, in front, and behind. And this discovery unnerved him greatly. He hadn't felt this disturbed since his wife had passed with cancer.

I have to look into this, he thought.

He left the sick animal and tended to the rest of the herd, using Maikoh to help him move the rest of the pack up the slope of the plateau, the sound of the hoppers crunching underfoot. The herd was obedient and looked tired in the afternoon sun as it slowly crawled up the hill, followed by Adam and Maikoh. The sheep were only too happy to reach the top of the hill, where Adam and his relatives had constructed a small ramada made of cottonwood. The ramada looked ragged, had several broken pieces, and leaned hard in one direction. The herd made its way under the ramada and settled down just as the sun was setting.

Adam gave his horse some hay from the little pile near his house and puzzled over the sick sheep. He didn't like the thought of losing one more animal. The herd supplied some of his income, but he had also taken a part-time job as a tour guide for Antelope Canyon. The canyon was one of the most visited and photographed tourist sites in the southwest.

He fixed himself some cornmeal and grabbed a cup of water from the twenty-gallon tank in his house, returned outside, and once again, mounted Maikoh.

Even though the sun had set, the thermometer on Adam's house read 129, and beads of sweat punctuated his brow.

Adam felt obligated to save the sickened sheep, and since he had no answer for the sickness, he decided to ride the mile and a half to his cousin's house and call the Navajo vet in Page, who was also an animal medicine man. The ride was necessary since Adam, preferring the old ways, chose not to own a phone or car. His cousin, Charly, also had a small herd of sheep and often helped him tend some of his crops or obtain water from the water tankers.

"Hello, brother," Charly Many Goats called as Adam approached Charly's small house.

"Good to see you, brother. I need your help."

As Adam stepped into Charly's house, he noticed again the coating of grasshoppers on the ground. Several had been stepped on and crushed by Charly's family.

"What brings you around?" Charly asked.

"I've got a sick sheep down by the river. Found it today. And it's strange, but I can't find any reason for it to be sick. No animal bites or injuries. It's just lying there, breathing heavily by the edge of the river. So I thought I'd better get the vet up in Page to come down and take a look."

"Sounds like a good idea."

"Have any of your animals become sick lately?" Adam asked his cousin.

"One was taken by a dog and dragged off last week. Seems to be happening more often. But none of them have really been sick. Just losing some weight and looking more dehydrated.

"But my wife, Delores, has been in the hospital in Tuba City. She took our herd down to the river yesterday to cool them off. She was so hot that she dunked herself in the water. I think she maybe picked up a parasite there, but they're not sure. She's been bringing up some blood from her throat, so I don't know. I'm kind of worried about her."

"I'm sorry. I hope she comes home soon. Can I use your phone?"

"Sure."

Adam borrowed Charly's phone and dialed the vet's number. He agreed to come down to Adam's house the next day.

Charly continued, "You know, Adam, we've been having trouble getting enough water lately. The little spring we use has all but dried up, so we're relying more on the water tankers."

"Yeah, I know. The Feds were supposed to help us with money to pipe some water from Page, but, shit, that never came."

JULY 13

ADAM'S HOUSE

AIR TEMP 108°F, 9:00 A.M.

"**THANKS FOR** coming down."

"Not a problem. I haven't been very busy lately. A lot of my clients have downsized their animal herds with the drought, and I've had to take on new clients up into southern Utah, as far as Kanab."

Ray Besty had practiced as a vet for fifteen years in Page and welcomed the opportunity to help a fellow Navajo.

"Where is your sheep?"

"He's down by the river."

Adam and the vet made their way down to the river, more grasshoppers landing on their backs.

After a while, they found the sheep.

"Is this the one you were talking about?" Ray asked.

"Yeah, I found him yesterday in the late afternoon, with some blood oozing out of his butt."

"Hmmm," Ray mumbled as he bent over to examine the animal. "You're right. No snake bite, coyote bites, or injuries. The abdomen's soft. Boy, he looks thin!"

The sheep was clinging to life, his ribs apparent in the morning light. The vet put his stethoscope on the animal's chest.

"His lungs sound a bit raspy, and there are some rough wheezes too."

The vet pulled out a thermometer and inserted it into the animal's rectum.

"Temp's normal. So no infection. You been feeding him any differently?"

"No, they're all eating less with the drought. Now and then I'll give them some extra hay."

"Was he acting sick before this?"

"No, just found him like this yesterday."

"Has he been drinking any water from other streams or rivers? I've found some other sheep sickened recently by poisonous algae in drying streams, but mainly in southern Utah."

"No, don't think so."

"Well, I want to draw some blood and send it to the lab. May give us some answers."

"OK."

"You want me to take him into the clinic and try to nurse him back?"

"Nah. Looks like he's had it. I can't afford it."

"OK. I'll call your cousin when the labs come back."

"Thanks again."

The vet placed the syringe into the sheep's neck and drew about 40 ccs of blood. The blood had a definite bluish hue. Then he put the sample into an ice pack he had brought with him.

The animal lay there quietly. Next the vet stepped into the river and felt the water. It appeared greenish. There was a definite green-brown sludge on top of the water as it slowly made its way down the channel.

"The river really feels warm today. Kinda smelly too."

"I know," Adam responded. "It's been like that for months now. Ever since they drained most of that dam up by Page, the river's been getting shallower and shallower. I guess that's why it's getting warmer. But it still lets the herd cool off a bit."

"You know, I've seen some parasitic infections in other sheep herds that drink from the river. May be a result of the warming. I'll check for those in the labs."

Before Adam and Ray began the climb back up the bank, Ray pulled a small sheepskin bag from his pocket. It contained pollen from one of the flowers that grew on the plateau. He pulled some grains and sprinkled them gently over the sheep. Then Ray spoke a short Navajo prayer for the animal. They climbed back up the bank to Adam's house.

"Should be about a day or two for the labs."

"Thanks again for coming out."

"No problem. Happy to do it."

Adam watched as the vet's old jeep started up the dirt road away from his house and disappeared over a hill.

Adam went inside his hogan, which was used mainly for spiritual purposes, and began a ritual to pray for the sheep.

JULY 15

ADAM'S HOUSE

AIR TEMP 111°F, 10:00 A.M.

ADAM WAS SITTING in his house sipping on some coffee when his cousin pulled up in his old Ford.

"Hello, brother."

"Hello, Adam."

"Come in. I've got some coffee for you."

Adam noted that Charly had a strange look on his wrinkled face, a mixture of concern and bewilderment.

As the two sat in the small kitchen area, Charly pulled a note from his shirt.

"I wrote down what the vet said about your sheep when he called this morning."

Adam fixed his gaze on his cousin.

Charly held the note in the morning light and began to read. "Labs are mostly normal. No parasitic infections or worms. Normal liver and kidney functions. White count is normal, so no infection. There is a huge decrease in the number of red cells in the animal's blood. That usually happens when the animal is severely injured, but we found no evidence of injuries. I can't explain this level of anemia with just malnutrition or heat. Let me know if the animal recovers. If not, I could autopsy it to look for other clues. No charge for a member of my clan."

Adam sat there and slowly took in the information. Hozho was, in his mind, still broken. Then he remembered his cousin's wife.

"Charly, how's Delores?"

"She passed yesterday, Adam."

"No! What happened? Why didn't you tell me?"

"I'm sorry, Adam. I've been too shaken up. They don't know why she died. No parasites, and she was healthy until now."

"Brother . . . I will say a special prayer for her."

The next day Adam's sheep died. As was the custom, Adam carried the old sheep to a small hill near his hogan, dug a deep hole, and buried the animal so the wild dogs could not find it. After this, he sadly went into his hogan and said a final prayer for the animal and for Charly's wife.

JULY 14

NEAR HAVASUPAI INDIAN RESERVATION

AIR TEMP 119°F, 11:00 A.M.

CARSON LEANED OVER the shallow bank, washed his face with the warm greenish river water, and cupped his hands for a drink. He was near the end of a morning hike at the bottom of the Grand Canyon and was so thirsty that he couldn't wait to get back to camp near the Havasupai Indian Reservation.

The Havasupai tribe lived near the bottom of the Canyon or on the North Rim. They had been there for eight hundred-some years. In the 1990s the tribe had begun to generate cash from tourists like Carson who booked tours into the base of the Canyon. Many hikers stayed overnight at a campground near the village of Supai. For years the tours would fill up six months ahead.

But in the early 2020s, business began to fade. The temperatures at the bottom of the Canyon climbed to nearly 128 degrees in the summer. It was always hotter at the bottom than at the top. There were two reasons for this phenomenon. One, the air temperature would increase by one degree for every 860-foot drop in elevation, making the bottom, on average, six or seven degrees warmer than the top. The second reason was more subtle. The Canyon itself acted as a wind break. Any wind from above that blew across the top of the Canyon would be redirected away from the depths, keeping the internal temps of the Canyon quite warm.

The thunderstorms that used to cool the Canyon every summer became fewer and fewer. In 2026, Arizona tried seeding the clouds with silver iodide. Sometimes that helped, but when the humidity dropped below 5 percent, this treatment couldn't squeeze much water from the scarce clouds.

Thus, the Havasupai tribal population near Supai and points east had dwindled to 450 in 2036. The COVID-19 pandemic in 2020 and succeeding years didn't help much, and the members had moved to cooler areas. The young ones had left long ago for larger cities, most of them heading to Vegas. They found employment in the many casinos. Some were also employed installing solar arrays in the bottom of Lake Powell.

Many of the remaining elders had moved to the cooler North Rim of the Canyon. Their houses were generally about 35–40 degrees cooler than the outside air, which could reach 126 or more in the summer. It had become too hot to grow their usual crops of corn and beans, so food had to come from a small town near the North Rim. Most afternoons they just napped inside their cool houses until the temperature fell enough to be comfortable. They passed their time carving juniper and cottonwood and also made clay pottery to sell to tourists. Most of them were over seventy now, and they waited to die in the vicinity of the Canyon, wanting to be buried with their ancestors.

Carson returned to the campground in the late morning and sat on his cot.

He coughed slightly. He heard other tourists in their tents coughing also. Even though the walls of the Canyon protected them from most of the dust that plagued visitors above, some of it still drifted down on occasion, particularly in the summer, when the ground above was bone dry. Carson couldn't remember the last rain that had occurred in the Grand Canyon. Maybe two years ago, and then only 1/16 of an inch at the most during the monsoon in August. He would stay one more night in the campground and then hike back up.

The next morning, before heading back up to the South Rim, he began to cough a lot. Must be the dust, he thought. He began to hike back up the trail with other tourists who had been staying in some of the Havasupai cabins. Everyone seemed to be coughing occasionally as they made their way back to the top.

JULY 16

HUALAPAI
TRIBAL AREA

AIR TEMP 120°F, 11:00 A.M.

CODY AND ALEX HAD MADE their way down the six-mile trail to the bottom of the Canyon. This trail was located northwest of the Hualapai Reservation. In 2007, the tribe had constructed the Grand Canyon Skywalk for tourists, a 980-square-foot clear platform on top of a curved cantilever bridge located forty-eight hundred feet above the bottom of the Canyon. Tourists came from every state and overseas to look below their feet almost one mile down into the Canyon. The hardened plexiglass was only six inches thick but held up to three tons of weight. Most people described the feeling as floating in the air above the Canyon. They readily paid the $650 fee for the view.

The tourism business had been doing well, and the tribe had begun charging for the use of its hiking trails down into the canyon. The tribe owned about fifteen hundred square miles of land adjacent to the south side of the canyon, 140 miles west of the visitor center at the South Rim.

Cody and Alex had come down into the Canyon on one of these trails. The morning they had left, it had broken 117 degrees Fahrenheit at the top. As they now stood near the Colorado River at the bottom, their pack gauge read 128°F. Sweat was pouring from their bodies, and they felt a little lightheaded from the heat.

They had brought ample water for their three-day trip and were well aware of the temperatures that could occur this time of the year. The hike had been planned in response to a challenge from a coworker, Miles, who had predicted that they couldn't finish a three-day hike in the July heat. However, they were veteran hikers and had hiked the Canyon many summers in the past. They had accepted the challenge, but now, as they were pitching their tent for the night, they wondered if it was worth it.

"I know the air temp reads 128 but it feels like 135 to me," Cody said.

"We must have gone through three gallons of electrolyte solution each today on the hike."

"I know. I'm beat," Alex agreed. "Maybe I should get some extra river water. If we're going to do that short four-miler tomorrow, then we'll need more water. We've used up a lot of water today on the way down."

"OK. Just be sure you use the iodine tabs we bought."

"Yeah, sure," Alex replied. "One per gallon, right?"

"Yeah, exactly."

Alex pulled the iodine from the pack and headed toward the river with four one-gallon water containers.

The river here was only about ninety feet wide and about five to six feet deep. It was much shallower and narrower since Lake Powell had nearly been drained. As Alex put his hand in the water, it felt unusually warm. Some greenish plant material floated on the surface. He took his water temperature gauge and dropped it in—100.4—higher than body temperature. He filled the containers with the warm liquid and headed back to camp. He used a filter to scour out the plant material, then placed one iodine tablet in each container, stirred them, and waited for two hours for the tablets to purify them.

Meanwhile, they finished pitching the two-man tent. Even with the heat, they were opting to sleep in the tent because they didn't want any critters joining them for the night. They laid out their air mattresses and prepared dinner—some freeze-dried stuff. After dinner, as the sun sank in the west, they could definitely feel the temperature begin to drop.

"I'm going to taste the treated water," Alex said. "Let's see if it's fit for tomorrow."

Using a canteen cup, he swallowed the still-warm water.

"Seems OK. Pretty warm, and I can still taste some

plant material, but it should be safe and cooler by tomorrow."

The Milky Way spread like a blanket across the sky. The moon rose above the Canyon in the east, shining as a pale sun. They both climbed in on top of the light mattresses. Gentle sounds of the night lulled them to sleep.

The next morning, they awoke about 6:00 a.m. and gathered stuff for the planned hike. Their route would take them a few miles farther along the edge of the river. They left the tent pitched, knowing they would sleep there again that night. They headed west in the early morning light.

About one mile out, Alex started to feel nauseated.

"Can't be the heat. The sun's barely up now, and I've been drinking every fifteen minutes. I hope it's not my gastritis again," he said. "I thought that was cured two months ago."

"Is it mainly your stomach?" Cody asked.

"Well, I feel some mild pain in my chest too."

"Really? You don't have heart problems, do you?"

"Not that I know of," Alex replied.

They continued for another half mile. The sun was now beating down on them from above the canyon edge. Alex began to cough. A long dry cough. And then he noticed some brownish mucus on his handkerchief.

"What the hell! I'm coughing up junk," he said.

"Are you still feeling sick?"

"Stomach's not too bad, but I'm beginning to feel a

little lightheaded. Could be the temperature."

"Maybe we should head back," Cody said, concerned.

"Yeah, might be a good idea. I hate to give up on our plans, but it's getting mighty hot. And I don't feel so good."

They turned around reluctantly and headed back down the trail.

"What's the temp now?" Alex asked.

"122 and climbing," Cody said.

When they made it back to the campground after about a mile and a half, Alex suddenly felt very strange.

"Let's get out of here. I know it's hot, but something's wrong," Alex said.

They quickly took their tent down, rested briefly for about fifteen minutes, drinking more of their water, and then began the long trek back up the original trail they had come down the day before. It took them about three hours in the heat. They were both sweating profusely. They were drinking from their electrolyte solution pouches every ten minutes or so. Every now and then, they would run across some other hikers who were headed down. The hikers, seeing Alex's condition, would offer them some more water. Even so, Alex had to take extra drinks from the water they had purified the night before.

By the time they reached the top, they were both exhausted. Alex had continued to cough up more brownish mucus and could barely walk.

"Got to be my gastritis," he said in a tired voice.

"Whatever, we're going to take you to the ER in Vegas," Cody said.

Alex didn't have the energy to protest. They both climbed into the Tesla and headed the 110 miles into south Las Vegas. Cody brought up the car's phone by voice command and alerted the ER in Vegas that they were coming.

When they reached the ER entrance, it was 7:30 p.m. and almost dark. A nurse met them at the door. She was one of the recent hires who had relocated from Phoenix.

She asked, "What's up? You guys look tired."

"My buddy's been coughing a little brownish junk all afternoon. We were hiking down in the Canyon and—"

Alex suddenly vomited and began coughing up some more brownish fluid.

"It's gotten worse in the last few hours," Cody told the nurse.

"How much stuff has he been coughing up?"

"I don't know, maybe a small cupful at least," Cody said worriedly.

"Any medical history? Ulcers, anticoagulants, gastritis, Crohn's, bronchitis, pneumonia?"

Alex replied, "I did have some gastritis about two months ago. The doc gave me some antibiotics and antacid pills for that *H. pylori* bacteria, but I've had no problems since then."

"OK, Dr. Singh will see you shortly."

Singh was another one of the doctors who had left

Phoenix. Most docs were leaving Arizona in droves, a product of the severe climate changes, rising housing prices, population decline, and water issues that had hit all the major cities in Arizona.

Singh arrived after a few minutes.

"Nicole filled me in on the history. I'm going to order some labs—CBCs, coags, cocci antibodies. Let's see what they show."

He listened to Alex's chest and headed off to another patient.

"See you in about twenty."

When Singh returned, Alex could see a puzzled look on his face.

"Nothing much. Borderline hemoglobin. Everything looks normal. No cocci either. We've been seeing more advanced cocci disease, due to the blowing dust, but you're negative."

"Hey, doc, what's cocci anyway?"

"It's Valley Fever. Coccidioidomycosis is a fungus that lives in the soil in the Southwest."

Singh poked on Alex's stomach.

"Any pain?"

"No."

"Good. OK, I'm going to order a GI consult anyway because of the brownish phlegm and your history of gastritis. Your chest X-ray was negative for any infections, but I suspect something possibly in your stomach. Maybe your gastritis has come back."

Thirty minutes later, the GI doctor on call, Dr. Mikelsen, entered the bay.

"Dr. Singh filled me in," she said. "Was your gastritis treated with standard therapy?"

"Yeah, I guess so. Three antibiotics, I think, tetracycline, Flagyl, and amoxicillin. I felt fine after that. But that was two months ago."

She poked on Alex's stomach area.

"Any pain?"

"No, not really."

"OK, I want to scope you here in the ER on an emergency basis. We need to rule out any other pathology in the stomach and esophagus. Your coughing could have dislodged some bleeders in the esophagus. An ulcer, or recurrent gastritis, is also possible. Do you drink? Any foreign travel? Sometimes parasites present this way."

"No."

"OK, I'll be back."

Ten minutes later she returned with the anesthesiologist on call. Alex was wheeled into another room. As the intravenous fentanyl took hold, Alex drifted off.

He awoke, groggy, twenty-five minutes later to see a blurry Dr. Mikelsen.

"Everything's clear, no sign of bleeds or recurrent gastritis in the stomach. Esophagus normal. So I'm not sure. Your chest X-ray was negative, so I suppose it could just be a small ruptured vessel we can't see. But I think we'll keep you overnight, just to be sure. I'll write a pulmonary and GI referral for when you get back to Phoenix."

Alex spent the night uneventfully. The coughing got better. The next morning, he and Cody climbed back into the Tesla and headed down US 93 to Phoenix.

BANNER EAST HOSPITAL, LAS VEGAS, NEVADA

AIR TEMP 121°F, 11:00 A.M.

MICHELLE SUNDSTROM, RN, adjusted her stethoscope as she listened to her patient.

"Sounds good. Looks like we'll be discharging you later today, as long as Dr. Begay agrees."

Michelle had been working at the new hospital for a year now. She enjoyed seeing every kind of medical patient and spent most days on the med-surg wards. The hospital had been constructed on the eastern side of Vegas, as part of Banner Health's expansion into the Nevada area. It boasted 290 beds, a new ER, and a state-of-the-art cancer center. The new hospital was fully staffed because Vegas, due to "the straw" into Lake Mead and deeper wells, had for the moment an ample supply of water. Most of the physicians and nurses who were leaving Arizona due to climate change and diminishing water supplies came to Vegas to continue their careers.

As she finished with her patient, Michelle started coughing. She had been getting bronchitis for four to five days now, and the cough had been getting naggingly worse. She finished her morning shift and headed down into the cafeteria area for lunch. It was always busy with staff. She got a sandwich, salad, and diet coke and settled down at a table near colleagues.

"Hey, Natasha, how's Peds?" Michelle asked.

"Oh, busy as usual. We got a new CF patient this morning, pretty low lung functions, so I'm watching her carefully. How have you been?"

"Mostly good. But I've got this damn bronchitis lately. Maybe it's the hours on med-surg, or maybe I'm getting it from the patients," Michelle replied. "I've been on the Z-pak for two days, and it seems to be helping."

"That's good," Natasha replied. "Z-pak usually works well for mild bronchitis."

"Yeah."

Michelle ate a bite of her sandwich, then coughed loudly, with a rasp. She looked at her napkin. Some yellow mucus streaked with a bit of brown covered one corner.

"Boy, I thought I was getting better. "

"Maybe you should go up to employee health and get it checked out," Natasha said.

"Yeah, I hear they got a new MD working there who's a sexy dude."

"Yeah, I heard that too. Good news travels fast."

Michelle left her friend and took the elevator to the third floor, where employees with minor illnesses and injuries were seen. The hospital used the employee health clinic to get employees treated quicker than they would otherwise on the outside.

The receptionist asked, "What's up?"

"I've had a bronchitis now for two or three days, I'm on the Z-pak, and I'm not getting any better."

"OK, let me get Dr. Melillo. He's new, but very experienced. He came up from Phoenix this year. He's boarded in occupational health and has lots of urgent care experience."

"Great."

The clinic was modestly full, but Melillo, thirty-seven, appeared quickly in her room and began taking the history. Michelle admired Melillo's physique and his rock-hard abs, created by weekends in the Red Rocks outside Vegas rock climbing.

"So, how long have you been sick?"

"It started five or six days ago with just a mild cough, no real temperature or chills, but today in the cafeteria, I just started coughing up some brownish mucus. I've been on a Z-pak now for two days, thought I was getting better, but I'm here."

"OK, we sometimes see this presentation with Valley

Fever. Have you been working in the desert, your garden, or involved in any archaeological sites?'

"The only thing I can think of is that I recently bought a new house, and they have just finished constructing it."

"Well, as you know, cocci is a bad actor sometimes, but mostly in patients with other problems, like cancer or diabetes, and you don't have any of those. But we'll check you for cocci anyway."

Melillo ordered the chest X-ray, a CBC, and cocci antibodies. The health center sported a new lab machine the size of a shoebox that could spit out most labs in only one minute.

The robot tech drew her blood and placed it into the lab machine. After ten minutes or so, Melillo came back.

"Huh. I'm not sure. Your chest X-ray is normal, except for a few tiny calcifications. Could just be an old infection. And your CBC was perfect. No cocci either. Any anticoagulants?"

"No."

"Using any aspirin or Motrin?"

"Not really. Just four hundred milligrams of Motrin this morning. That's usually all I take for stress headaches."

"Could be you just got some minor broken blood vessels in the throat or bronchi from the coughing," he said. "I'm going to switch you to Zybranc, send you home to rest, and let's see you back here in three days. If it's just from coughing, then the rest and meds should help."

"OK, doc. See you in a few days."

Michelle followed the doctor's orders and came back three days later. Melillo was on shift that day.

"How are you?"

"Better. The mucus stopped after only one day. And I feel fine now."

"Great. Finish the Zybranc and you should be able to go back to work this Thursday."

Michelle watched him write the discharge orders and again admired his slim, hard body.

JULY 18

BANNER EAST HOSPITAL, LAS VEGAS

AIR TEMP 123°F, NOON

VINCE SAUNDERS had been a patient at Banner East Las Vegas since his lung cancer had been diagnosed two weeks earlier. He was forty-eight, married, had two children, and had lived east of Vegas for the last twenty years. Even though he had been a heavy smoker (three packs a day for twenty years), he, like many other smokers, had never expected to become a lung cancer patient.

He had chosen Banner East and Dr. Chen for their expertise. The new cancer center at Banner East boasted several regimens for treating cancer—a new cyber knife, high wattage laser, proton beam radiation, and the latest chemotherapy and individualized biomolecular regimens. His cancer was initially found on a routine chest X-ray, and his treatment began immediately. His disease was confined to a small area of his left lower lobe and diagnosed as small cell lung cancer. He received three days of proton beam radiation, then underwent surgery to remove the three-centimeter mass. All surrounding nodes were negative. The cancer cells in the tumor mass had their DNA sequenced at the hospital, a process that took only a few hours. DNA sequencing of tumors had been the gold standard for fifteen years now, and sometimes the sequences showed new mutations that were susceptible to specific cancer medicines. The newer DNA sequencers spit out their data in hours versus the weeks it used to take in the old days.

Vince hoped that they could find something new that could ultimately be treated. But Chen knew from experience that cancer was a sometimes-baffling opponent, and not all of his patients would survive. In spite of several new therapies in 2036, still fully 10–20 percent of Vince's type of lung tumor led to death. It was a similar solid tumor that Stone was attempting to cure with his nanomachine. But since Stone's research trial with the nanobot had not been finished or published, Chen was unaware of it.

Later that day, Vince anxiously greeted Chen as he entered his room with the results.

"What did you find?"

"Well, you have some new mutation sequences, a

couple that are susceptible to some common agents, and one we've never seen before."

Chen was known for being blunt, but then his specialty demanded it.

"What does that mean?" Vince asked cautiously.

"It means that the ones we've seen before will probably respond well to standard agents, but we're going to have to try some really new therapies for the unusual mutation."

Chen had been an oncologist for twenty-five years and was versed in all the latest drug and biomolecular treatments. He was used to putting on a hopeful face for patients but also tried to be totally honest when it came to predicting life or death.

"I'll level with you, Vince. This time, I'm not so sure. We'll do our best. I'm going to consult with colleagues at MD Anderson in Houston about the new mutation and the best approach for it."

Banner East had a direct link through the internet to the latest treatments and research, and in addition, Chen could talk directly to any cancer specialist in the country.

"I'll check the experimental literature today, call MD Anderson, and get back to you in a few hours. By the way, you'll need some more hydration fluids before we start the new treatment. These latest therapies can be pretty toxic, and hydrating will save you a few side effects."

As Chen left the room, Vince's initial hope waned a bit. He immediately thought of his family. He would have to talk to Jenn, his wife of twenty years, right away. His two sons also deserved to know the odds.

Vince's RN, Lissette, was a veteran of seven years on the cancer wards, having transferred to Vegas from Phoenix five years earlier. She had worked with many cancer patients and seen every possible outcome. She had seen newer treatments succeed, but also fail. But she had faith in Chen, who sometimes came up with the most bizarre, but also the most successful, treatments.

As Lissette replaced Vince's IV bag of normal saline, she recalled her last patient, a thirty-eight-year-old female with early ovarian cancer. After surgery, she was given two experimental agents, one of which caused her to grow strange benign tumors all over her body so that she looked like the Elephant Man. But the treatments ultimately led to a cure.

Now, as she attended to Vince, she had full faith in Chen. He was sometimes referred to as "the Wizard" by other oncologists at Banner for his creativity in the face of overwhelming odds and his willingness to experiment with different therapies.

Chen came back later that day. He looked optimistic, but then he was an expert at not alerting patients to his emotions.

"Vince, I've just looked at MD Anderson's latest recommendations for your type of cancer, and I've spoken to their top oncologist. I've chosen two new drugs—one is a brand-new checkpoint inhibitor. A checkpoint inhibitor is a drug that releases killer T cells to fully express themselves against cancer. If that doesn't give results, we'll send some of your lymphocytes to our oncology lab here to become CAR T cells, or killer T cells, which are programmed to attack your specific tumor. But we have to administer them in unusually high doses, and therefore you'll need a lot of fluids while under treatment."

"What is the chance all this will work?" Vince asked hopefully.

"If I was a gambling man, which I'm not, then I'd say 55 percent chance of success. But these are mostly untried therapies. You'll have some major side effects—maybe extra bleeding at the site of the tumor, maybe some skin growths. But these should be manageable."

"OK, when do we start?"

"Later today. They're already flying in the first meds from Houston."

"OK. Thanks, doc."

As soon as he heard of the plan, Vince felt a little more optimistic. At least they were starting soon. Lissette ordered the fourth liter of saline that day.

"Let's get you fluid overloaded, Vince," she said. "I want you to drink as much water and other fluids as you can. You'll pee a lot, but I want you ready for the new meds when they get here."

Late in the afternoon, the treatments arrived. Lissette hung the new drug immediately. The IV bags were a funny, orange-green color. She had expected something different, but the color was weird. She had to mix the solution in a ventilated hood because of its toxicity.

For the first few days, Vince struggled with nausea and vomiting, but then settled a bit.

On the third day after receiving the checkpoint inhibitor, he began to vomit up a small amount of blood, about a teaspoon full. Chen wasn't worried, as the experts at MD Anderson had predicted this side effect from the new medicine. But the next day, he really began to bleed more, and then that afternoon, he started to cough up larger gobs of blood.

Chen dialed the meds down a bit, but the bleeding continued. They ended up giving him five extra units of blood, but Vince went into a coma and died on the fourth day, with massive bleeding from his mouth. The CAR T-cell therapy went untried.

Vince's death was discussed in the M&M (morbidity and mortality) conference the next day. His pathology report after the autopsy showed an excessive amount of hemorrhaging in the normal lung tissue around the tumor and also from other lobes of both his left and right lung, a result that couldn't be completely explained by the new agents. As per standard protocol, his death report was filed with the Southern Nevada Health District.

JULY 18

NELLIS AIR FORCE BASE, LAS VEGAS

AIR TEMP 114°F, 0800

NATHAN CARTER, captain, US Air Force, pulled back on the stick of his F40 as it ran down runway 23B at Nellis. He was a fifteen-year veteran fighter pilot who had trained on the F40 at Luke Air Force Base west of Phoenix and had fought in the short Iran War that the country had stumbled into in 2025.

He quickly accelerated the jet to 600 mph with 2 g's on him and climbed to twenty thousand feet. His mission was combat training with his F40 group. Today two other pilots in F40s, playing the roles of Russian high-performance Slacker MiG-27s, were involved in the mission. The main objective was to test Carter's long-distance radar, which could detect enemy aircraft or missiles from 175 miles out. Two jets were now coming at him from north of Vegas at 1,000 mph.

"OK, I have you acquired," Carter told the two bandits. "I see you on my visor—range 140 miles. Estimated time to contact, three minutes."

Captain Carter accelerated his plane to 1,300 mph or Mach 1.8 and anticipated the closing altitude of 30,000 feet.

As he accelerated, now experiencing 4 g's, he noticed some mild lightheadedness. Two days earlier, he had been seen for a mild cold in the base health unit by an Air Force flight physician prior to returning to flight duty. The doctor had cleared him for flight status today, so the lightheadedness came as a surprise. The doctor had also advised hydrating a lot to clear the cold, so Carter had drunk a lot of fluids the day before at home and on the base.

As he reached 25,000 feet, the dizziness worsened, and he began to cough. The thin air at this altitude was extremely dry, which might explain the cough, but it worried him. He adjusted his oxygen percentage to 85 percent and upped his humidity, but the cough persisted. And then he noticed a small streak of grayish-brown mucus in his helmet faceplate as he coughed.

The F40's helmet was made of hardened plexiglass and allowed the pilot nearly 270 degrees of vision. It doubled as a virtual reality screen, so the pilot could read airspeed, altitude, and even radar images by looking through it. Some of the combat pilots had even elected to have chips implanted in their superficial cortex so they could perceive the same data directly into their brain.

"What the . . . hell," Carter said. "Base, I'm experiencing a funny cough."

"OK, Carter. What's your position in relation to the bandits?"

"Two minutes out, ninety-five miles."

"OK, any other problems?"

"Yeah, quite dizzy"

"Have you upped your oxygen?"

"Yes, no effect. And I'm coughing more. I'm feeling really lightheaded."

"OK, suggest return to base. We'll notify bandits."

"Copy that. Returning to base."

Nellis traffic control broke over the radio: "Bandits, Carter returning to base with health issue. May want to follow him back into Nellis."

"Copy, base, contact in one minute. Will intercept Carter."

But as Carter throttled back to 800 mph and turned toward Nellis at ten thousand feet, he suddenly began shaking wildly and then passed out. At five thousand feet, the automatic eject feature shot the unconscious Carter out of the aircraft.

"Bandits to base—over contact area, and we don't see Carter. There is a large plume of smoke below. Diving to investigate."

The two F40s flew down over the black smoke, and

as they got closer, they could see the remains of Carter's jet lying in the center of a large crater. They had seen no parachute.

"Base, seeing what appears to be crash site of Carter's jet. No survivors seen."

"OK, return to base. We'll send rescue."

The chopper rescue team took only five minutes to reach the crash site.

The large plume of smoke was clearly visible for miles. As they landed, they could see that the jet had come in at a very steep angle and quite a high speed. They climbed out of the chopper and cautiously examined the wreckage, still burning.

Then they found a small part of Carter's plexiglass face mask along with the crumpled remains of Carter a few hundred yards from the wreckage. The entire inside of the mask was coated with bright red blood. It was apparent to the rescuers that Carter's emergency chute had not opened.

"Shit. Not much left of him. Must've hit his head in the crash."

"Yeah, you would expect that," the other chopper pilot said.

Per Air Force protocol with unexplained crashes, his remains were collected and autopsied at Nellis, and pathology slides were sent out to Wright-Patterson AFB near Dayton, Ohio. A report was prepared, and slides were taken of all major organs and tissues that remained after the crash, including heart and lungs, even though very little remained of Carter. They could fit what was left of him in a small food bag.

AUGUST 1

WRIGHT PATTERSON AFB, DAYTON, OHIO

AIR TEMP 109°F, 9:00 A.M.

AIR FORCE MAJOR Alicia Hernandez, MD, was examining a high-magnification slide of Captain Nathan Carter's lung when she saw signs of unusual alveolar destruction and excessive red blood cell damage. Human lungs contain around three hundred million alveoli, the small bags at the end of lung bronchioles that process oxygen in and CO_2 out of the bloodstream with each breath. She immediately sent the slides to electron microscopy. Later that morning, the microscopist, Major Paula Galli, called her on the phone,

"Hey, Alicia. I've got Carter's slides on the scope. Come take a look."

Alicia crossed the street to the scanning electron

microscopy lab and peered at the section now being magnified some one million times.

"What do you think, Alicia?"

"Huh. Don't know. It's hard to make out, even at this magnification. But it looks like he may have had some kind of lung procedure. Did he have any bronchoscopies, tissue transplants—any lung stents or monitors placed? It's pretty common now to have this type of technology. If they ruptured, that could have caused the damage to the cells."

"Yeah, don't see anything in his records. Maybe the force of the crash caused the damage."

"Sounds good to me."

Paula turned off the scope.

Per protocol, the electron microscope report was signed by Major Galli and Major Hernandez and sent back to Nellis to be presented at the inquest. The final determination: air pilot loss of consciousness—reason unknown.

JULY 20

BULLHEAD CITY, ARIZONA

AIR TEMP 130°F, 5:00 P.M.

ANGELA BERG had just come home from her work as an accountant for a small manufacturing company in Bullhead City. Angela and Harrison Berg had lived there for the last ten years, since moving from Minneapolis. Like a lot of midwesterners, they wanted to escape the cold winters. Angela had hoped to improve her asthma and allergies, but, as many transplants quickly learned, Arizona's warm year-long growing season made allergy conditions worse. In particular, the tamarisk trees that grew along the banks of the Colorado were notorious for causing allergic reactions.

Angela had made the trip to her allergist in Las Vegas many times, and she had been prescribed a regimen of daily Montelukast, a mast cell stabilizer, Albuterol as needed, and daily nebulizer treatments.

After supper, Angela started one of her neb treatments. She filled the nebulizer with steroid solution and water and began to breathe from it. After ten minutes or so, her breaths came easier.

"I'm using more water in my neb solution now," she told her husband, "and that seems to be helping more."

"OK, honey. I'm glad."

Harrison, a decade older than Angela, was retired and spent most days on the golf course or hiking in the nearby Black Mountains.

Before bed, Angela took another neb treatment and climbed in.

At 6:00 a.m. Harrison awoke to Angela coughing.

"You sure you nebbed enough last night?" he asked.

"Yes, twice. Once after supper and once before bed."

"What's that on your pillow?"

As Angela glanced to her right, she saw a small brownish splotch on the pillow.

"It looks like junk from my throat. Maybe from coughing. Did I cough during the night.?"

"Yeah. A little."

As Harrison watched, Angela began to cough in large spasms. They became so bad, she had to get out of bed and go into the bathroom.

"Maybe you should do another treatment," Harrison suggested.

"I think you should call an ambulance. I can't stop coughing, and I'm beginning to feel dizzy."

As Harrison watched in horror, his wife gave a large gasp and several tablespoons of brownish gunk squirted from her mouth onto the bathroom floor. She stumbled back into the bedroom and collapsed.

A terrified Harrison cried out, "What's wrong? Angela! Oh my God!"

Harrison stumbled out of bed, ran to Angela, and felt for her breathing and pulse. There was no pulse, but a small current of air escaped from her mouth. A small pool of brownish phlegm had now formed on the bedroom tile. Harrison ran to the phone, called 911, and began CPR.

Four minutes later, the ambulance arrived from the nearest hospital, which was six miles away. The EMT continued CPR, quickly surveying the scene.

"What happened?"

"She had a coughing spasm with some brownish phlegm coming out," Harrison hurriedly told him. "She has a history of bad asthma, is getting albuterol and neb treatments, but I've never seen anything like this with her."

"Any anticoagulants or aspirin? Any history of cocci?"

"Yeah, she is on one baby aspirin a day for her heart."

The EMT continued CPR for one more minute, felt for a pulse, found none, hung a line quickly, injected epinephrine, and placed Angela on the cart. His partner continued CPR. They quickly put her into the ambulance.

They arrived at the ER entrance, but in spite of three epinephrine doses and three shocks, Angela had already expired on the way.

JULY 21

PARKER DAM, LA PAZ COUNTY, ARIZONA

AIR TEMP 124°F, 10:00 A.M.

HOLDEN AND BRENT THOMAS had come from Phoenix to tour the Parker Dam, having toured both Hoover Dam and Glen Canyon Dam several months earlier. The brothers were interested in following the water situation in Arizona, which had become dicey recently.

Since the partial destruction of the Glen Canyon Dam in 2023, Lake Mead behind Hoover Dam continued to supply water to Las Vegas, southern California, and points south in Arizona. The Central Arizona Project, or CAP, which had been completed in 1993 at a cost of $4 billion, continued to pump water from the Colorado River twenty-four hundred feet upward from Lake Havasu, the reservoir behind Parker Dam, into western

Arizona, then on into Phoenix and ultimately Tucson. Phoenix and Tucson had seen their supply of CAP water cut drastically since the DCP expired in 2026. Bickering in the state capitol and fights between the large cities in Arizona and the farmers in rural counties continued ten years later. Normally, cities like Phoenix and Tucson would get what they wanted in terms of water. But after the DCP expired, these cities had their CAP water cut by 30 percent or more. At the time, the farmers had demanded $30 million for digging deeper wells and got it.

Small cities along the Colorado's route, like Lake Havasu City, just north of Parker Dam, did not have the clout of Phoenix and Tucson. However, they and other small cities around the state continued to get only a small amount of water from the Colorado. As a result, most smaller cities relied even more on deep wells.

Holden and Brent looked forward to the tour that day. The Parker Dam, after being retrofitted with new turbines, still supplied a small amount of power to Blythe and Palm Springs. The brothers learned that the dam generated just short of 120 megawatts of power most of the time. The main pumping station for the CAP was located next to the dam. Because of the station's importance, the politicians always funded needed projects there, like the recent update to the turbine generating plant.

At the start of the tour, the brothers took the steps down into the turbine room, where they saw the four new small turbines, each generating 30 megawatts. Each of the turbines was spinning rapidly after being fed by the intake towers from above. The dam itself measured 860 feet across and 320 feet high and once stored 210 million gallons of water.

"Take a good look at those turbines," the tour guide said. "They won't spin forever."

"Why not?" asked Holden.

"Well, Mead continues to fall to levels not seen before, and we depend solely on the water from Mead. The powers that be continue to cut the supply that is released downstream from Mead with the continuing drought, and I don't know how long we've got until deadpool."

Holden and Brent learned that deadpool means the water level behind a dam is no longer deep enough to supply any further water downstream. In addition, long before deadpool, the turbines would not have enough water pressure to generate electricity. Eventually, it seemed to the brothers that Parker Dam, like Glen Canyon before it, and even Hoover Dam, would ultimately reach deadpool.

After the tour and lunch, the brothers headed east to Cattail Cove at Lake Havasu State Park, a popular tourist destination. They had swim gear and hoped to cool off in the afternoon heat. The temperature gauge on Holden's Honda read 131 degrees Fahrenheit.

"Dude, I can't wait to get into that water."

"Shit, I know. But you realize it's 131 outside, so the water is going to be wa-a-arm, don't you?"

"Yeah, but anything is cooler than 131."

Holden and Brent parked the Honda, changed in the bathhouse, and ran into the water. The warm water temperature shocked them, but indeed it felt at least a little cooler than the air, and they got some evaporative cooling from a brisk breeze.

There were only a few tourists on the beach. Most had left for the day. A few powerboats plied the waters above the dam.

"Aw, this still feels good, even though that sign said, 'Water Temp 100.8,'" Brent said.

They tried to dunk each other but only succeeded in both swallowing large gulps of water, particularly Holden. They swam around for a few minutes, but the warm water wasn't that refreshing.

"Bro, after all of this warm water, I'm needing a beer," Holden said.

They dried off in the afternoon sun, which took about thirty seconds in the blazing heat, and headed for the car.

They soon found a bar down by Hillcrest Bay, which was packed with tourists who were hoping to cool off with cold drinks.

"Give me a cold one and maybe an electrolyte special," Holden said to the bartender.

"OK, coming right away."

They drank two electrolyte specials quickly, chugging the high sodium- and potassium-laden fluids, which slowly recharged their systems.

"What do you say we stay the night in Lake Havasu City and then explore the London Bridge tomorrow morning?"

"Awesome. I've heard a lot about that, but I've never seen it except on my streaming service."

They got back in the Honda and drove the thirty-eight miles to Lake Havasu City just as the sun was setting. They pulled up to a motel that advertised itself as "The London Bridge." They registered, grabbed a dinner from the motel's restaurant, and went to their room, where, after posting their latest photos to their social media accounts, fell asleep by 10:00 p.m.

JULY 22

LAKE HAVASU CITY, ARIZONA

AIR TEMP 121°F, 9:00 A.M.

ONE OF THE MOST POPULAR tourist spots in Lake Havasu City was London Bridge, which in 1967 had been disassembled in London brick by brick, transported to Arizona, and reassembled there. Although recent climate change and high temperatures had diminished the area's popularity, the Bridge was still the main tourist attraction in the area. The outflow from Hoover Dam and Lake Mead had been cut back to about 35 percent of what the flow had been in the early 2020s. Lake Havasu itself had shrunk by about 40 percent but was still large enough for tourists to enjoy.

Even so, the temperature extremes were becoming nearly intolerable. In the early 2020s, summer temps along the lake could reach 119 or more, but in the mid-2030s they were hitting well above 128 and even above 130 on occasion.

Holden and Brent slept in until 9:00 a.m. and headed down to the motel restaurant. Brent glanced at his phone.

"It says we're still under the control of that huge high-pressure ridge that came into Arizona over a week ago. Says they're expecting no relief for another few days, and today we may hit 132!"

"Yeah, I heard about that before we left Phoenix, that they were expecting a large rise over the average summer temperatures during the week. Maybe we should get going before it really gets hot today if we want to see that London Bridge."

"OK, I'll pay the bill."

The two walked out of the restaurant and headed for the bridge, which could easily be seen a few streets down. A few tourists were gathered at its base. The brothers headed up the west side of the bridge. Already, the sun felt pretty hot and it was only 10:00 a.m. The height of the late July sun made things worse. They grabbed two cool electrolyte drinks from a vending machine at the base of the bridge. A sign read, "Summer Temps May Reach 129 or More. Danger of Dehydration When on Bridge More than 20 Minutes. Recommend Extra Electrolyte Hydration. Cooling Vests Highly Recommended over 126 Degrees."

They ignored the advice about cooling vests and

began to climb the gradual slope at the base of the bridge.

"Let's see if we can get some good photos," said Brent.

"Yeah, good idea."

As they approached the center of the bridge, Holden began to slow down.

"You know, I don't feel so good."

"What's wrong?" Brent asked.

"I don't know, maybe it's the sun, but I feel light-headed and a little dizzy. More tired than usual too."

"Take another electrolyte drink. It's pretty hot."

Holden slugged his last drink and then started to cough. First, it was just a little cough, but then harsher, with a funny sound.

"Crap. Must be the dry heat and the temperature," Holden said.

They continued on, and Brent told Holden to stop when they were about halfway along the bridge. The morning sun was causing both to sweat profusely.

Holden carefully positioned himself along the edge of the bridge so Brent could get a good shot of him, the lake, and the bridge. He climbed up onto the stone railing and then, for the photo, carefully sat on the edge. Brent backed off a little, and was adjusting the focus on his cell when Holden called out,

"Bro, I feel, uhhh . . ." The sentence would not be completed.

As Brent looked quickly back to his brother, he caught a glimpse of Holden falling backward over the railing into the lake below. Horrified, Brent ran to the edge, just in time to see Holden splash into the water. His brother was a good swimmer, but as Brent looked down into the water, he saw no movement.

"Holden, little bro . . . hold on. . . . I'm going to get help," yelled Brent.

There was no response from the lake.

Brent punched 911 into his cell.

"Help, my brother just fell over the edge of the London Bridge! Hurry!"

"Can he swim?" the dispatcher asked.

"Yes, but I don't see him moving. He hit the water pretty hard."

"OK, we'll send someone immediately."

The 911 desk in Lake Havasu was used to this situation, as a fair number of tourists had fallen into the lake previously because of being too zealous about taking a photograph. They even had a nickname for it: a "killfie." In fact, in the past year, five other people had fallen in, and two had drowned.

As Brent kept an eye on Holden, he could still see no movement, just his brother barely floating silently on the surface. He didn't know how long it would take to get help, so, being a good swimmer himself, Brent climbed up onto the railing and dove in toward Holden. The few other tourists on the bridge looked on with concern and some ran up to where Brent had dived in and offered to help.

Brent swam to Holden and discovered to his horror that his brother was no longer breathing. He noticed a small pool of blood around his head.

Shit! I wonder if he hit his head on a rock, Brent thought to himself.

Brent immediately began to give Holden some breaths, being careful not to move his neck too much.

By then, the ambulance had arrived. Brent yelled to the EMTs and waved his free arm. The rescue team quickly drove to the side of the bridge. They inflated an instant raft, then began rowing out to the two men. When they arrived, they noticed a large amount of dark blood that appeared to be pooled on the surface just around his head.

"What do you make of that?" yelled one of the rescuers as they quickly pulled Holden onto the raft and took over CPR.

"Probably hit his head on a rock or something."

"Yeah, I guess. We've seen that before. The lake's not very deep here."

As the EMTs continued to work on him, Holden appeared unconscious, and bright red blood continued to flow from his head and mouth. A pulse check revealed nothing. When they reached the shore, a line was started. They administered epi once and then sped to the ER.

Brent swam to shore, hailed a rideshare, and followed them to the ER. He ran inside, and when he saw his brother on the gurney, he became terrified. Holden's face had turned slightly blue, and blood continued to ooze from him. Brent started to scream.

"Oh my God, no! He's still alive, isn't he?"

"I'm very sorry, he expired a few minutes ago," replied the ER doc who had just pronounced Holden dead moments before.

Brent began to cry in long, deep sobs. Holden was his only brother and his best friend in the world. The whole thing seemed like a bad dream. If only we hadn't tried to get that damn photo, he thought.

"I don't get it," the doc continued. "I'm not sure why he had so much bleeding. Did he have any medical problems?"

Brent replied haltingly through his sobs, "I do remember. . . . He was on an anticoagulant for his heart. . . . He did get a heart stent last year . . . but this cardiologist in Phoenix . . . had cleared him for any activity . . . including swimming."

"OK, that might explain the bleeding. He was bleeding quite a lot when the EMTs found him. He might have hit a submerged rock also. We'd like to autopsy him. Just a protocol we have here."

"No. I don't want him cut into. I just want to take him home."

"Well, in that case, let us know where you want his body taken. I'm really sorry about this, man. I know this isn't easy." The doc put a hand on Brent's shoulder.

"Well, we're from Phoenix. I'll have to call my sister-in-law. We'll have to get him transported back to Phoenix. I'll let you know when I know more."

Brent walked out of the ER still sobbing. He loved his only brother very much, and now he would have to bury him. I can't fucking believe this, he thought.

JULY 22

BANNER DENVER WEST RESEARCH CENTER

AIR TEMP 121°F, 5:00 P.M.

IT HAD BEEN OVER A WEEK since Stone had injected the first patient in the nanobot trial. He had been spending his time watching the techs injecting other patients, monitoring their responses, and answering their many questions about the tiny nanomachine design and function. So far, no serious problems or side effects had developed in the study participants, and he was happy about that.

He was in the provider lounge sipping on a cup of coffee when he glanced at the local news station feed on the virtual TV. The news crawl read, "Phoenix tourist drowns in Lake Havasu attempting to get selfie on London Bridge."

As he continued to read the details of the story, it reminded him of the young woman who had fallen to her death at Horseshoe Bend while attempting to take a selfie.

Stone thought to himself, Jeez, another selfie death! What's wrong with these kids!

The news also reminded him of the lost bots and $6 million down the drain. He shrugged and figured the bots had made a nice expensive meal for some fish.

JULY 22

ALONG THE
CAP CANAL

AIR TEMP 129°F, 2:00 P.M.

SECURITY GUARD BRANDON GAGE walked along the top of the Central Arizona Project canal twenty miles east of Lake Havasu City. The canal rose twenty-four hundred feet from its beginning near Parker Dam on its way east toward Phoenix. He was swatting two-inch, gray-brown grasshoppers off his cooling vest and shirt. There were so many, they were floating like a mat on top of the water. This was nothing new, as for months the grasshoppers had been devouring most of the crops in the more rural areas of Arizona. After reaching the Buckskin Mountains, the CAP canal headed east-north-east toward Wickenburg, southeast to Lake Pleasant, and then into the northern suburbs of Phoenix. The CAP had taken twenty years to construct and had cost $4 billion. Prior to the near draining of Lake Powell, it had delivered about half of the Valley's water needs. It was operated remotely at a facility in north Phoenix.

Along the way there were thirteen pumping stations, but the stations just east of Lake Havasu held the biggest pumps since they had to carry water out of the Colorado and up eight hundred feet into the desert. Since Lake Powell had been almost drained in 2023, the canals held less water than ever before. Phoenix was receiving only about 35 percent of what it had been receiving in the early 2020s.

The CAP canal was regularly patrolled on foot and with drones for any terrorists who might try to poison or contaminate the water. This was a tough job, given that the canal was 336 miles long. Twice daily, samples of the CAP water were taken and tested in a lab back in Phoenix.

There were newer problems too. Since the temperatures had reached 128 degrees in summer, the desert east of Lake Havasu had become more and more parched. The dust storms that had begun to plague Phoenix in the early 2010s had become much worse and more frequent. Sometimes clouds of grasshoppers were combined with the dust.

As a result, the usual clear water in the canals had become muddy brown with the dust from these storms. A retractable canal cover had been constructed to take care of this problem for the 140 miles of canal just west of Phoenix. And the pumps along the canal were having to work harder because of the high temps, particularly in the summer. The schedule of routine maintenance now included frequent overhauling of the pumps.

Gage walked slowly along the top of the canal and remembered Phoenix, his hometown, as it was in the 2020s, before Powell was nearly drained and before increasing global warming had changed everything.

In 2020, metropolitan Phoenix had boasted a population of 4.9 million, had become the fifth-largest city by population, and had the country's fifth-largest airport by passengers. Every year, at least seventy-five thousand immigrants came from other states into Maricopa County, fleeing their own water problems. Two-thirds of them came from California, where housing prices had become astronomical and forest fires had burned large swaths of the state. The air quality in Phoenix was reasonably good, despite the newcomers, and water was dirt cheap. The city had about twenty major universities and colleges.

The economy was booming, with high tech, health care, and business jobs so plentiful most employers had trouble filling their positions. With the influx of new residents, the rents in the city were sky-high, and housing prices had appreciated to almost unaffordable levels. Business leaders and state government were so focused on the hot economy that they downplayed the fact that Arizona was twenty years into a serious drought. The two reservoirs, Mead and Powell, were about 38 percent full, but the state legislature postponed addressing the climate change problem, with vocal opponents stating, "The rains will come; climate change is a hoax."

Gage was aware that for many years, scientists and conservationists had pleaded with state leaders to start a desalinization plant in the Gulf of California and simultaneously increase water conservation. Their suggestions fell on deaf ears, as the state legislature was loathe to increase any taxes on the citizens of Arizona even though California and Nevada were willing to contribute. In fact, California had already started to construct desalinization plants at several of its cities.

In late 2019, the first shortage declaration on the Colorado River had come from the Feds. The Drought Contingency Plan was signed, but it wasn't intended to solve the long-term problems of overallocation of the Colorado River and lack of a new supply.

Gage remembered that in 2020, the SARS-CoV-2 global pandemic infected over five hundred thousand Arizonans. The economy of the state took a huge hit, and, in Gage's opinion, the governor rushed to reopen too soon. A second and third wave hit the state, killing thousands more. It took a full two years for the economy to recover. Even though scientists around the world worked full-time, a vaccine wasn't ready for widespread use until late 2021. Because SARS-CoV-2 preoccupied everyone at the time, no one worried much about the water situation.

In 2022, dust from the former Salton Sea, some 260 miles west of Phoenix, began to blow east, carrying tons of arsenic and lead with it from the dry lake bed.

Several thousand Phoenix children developed brain damage from the toxins.

Gage well recalled the effects of the second shortage declaration on the river in 2024. People started to take notice, especially farmers in the south, some of whom had to close their farms. Property values began to dive, and water prices skyrocketed. The city wells had dropped to 1,700 feet, and the aquifer below the Valley of the Sun had been nearly tapped out. The metropolitan area then stood at 3.5 million residents and dropping.

Arizona Public Service, the main utility, kept running natural gas plants and one nuclear plant, but it had discouraged clean solar from the start, so there was no major solar backup for the energy supplying the city. Dust storms were a regular occurrence, turning the skies brown and sometimes lasting for days. The air quality had rapidly diminished, and Phoenix was now in 2024 second-worst in the country. As a result, the incidence of dust-related illnesses rose—especially asthma, and then coccidioidomycosis, or Valley Fever. Gage recalled with irony that, after many people fought over whether to wear masks for political reasons during the COVID-19 pandemic, people started wearing them again, but this time the reason was dust.

Air quality wasn't the only thing affected. Because

of high temperatures in the middle of the day, planes sometimes could land only at night, or they had to be diverted to other airports. The thin air at high temps could not supply enough lift for their weight. And when the dust storms rolled in, as they often did, the planes were diverted to Flagstaff, Vegas, and points north until the storms abated. Gage had been on a plane himself that had been diverted to Flagstaff, but at least by then they had built the magnetic highway between Flagstaff and Phoenix.

Valley Fever spores had caused a minipandemic of sorts in 2024. The cocci fungus spores lived in hibernation just below the surface of the desert soil. If inhaled into the lungs, the spores could quickly divide and cause serious illness. Some who inhaled the fungus came down with debilitating pneumonias, and many died, including Gage's uncle. The fungus was picked up on the wind and carried many miles. Gage remembered 2024 had been particularly bad for dust. Even those who worked in offices became infected, and virtually 100 percent of Phoenix residents had cocci antibodies in their blood by the time the pandemic was over. In that one year, seventy-five thousand residents had come down with the disease, and twenty-five thousand of them had been hospitalized, causing a drain on health resources similar to the problems experienced with COVID-19. Most citizens in Phoenix spent most of their days indoors, trying to avoid the heat and the bad air quality.

By the time the DCP expired in 2026, the city had already lost over one million people, mostly to the Northwest states, where abundant water still remained. Gage himself had moved out of the city to Lake Havasu by then. Businesses vanished, unable to keep up with the rising cost of water and other supplies. Farms and dairies failed in the south, and food and water had to be trucked in. Housing prices plummeted. The reservoirs east of Phoenix, owned by the Salt River Project and supplying 40 percent of the city's needs, kept up with demand for a while, but with the extended drought, even they eventually began to dry up. Phoenix quickly exhausted the recharged 4.6 million acre-feet that it had stored underground over the years, and deeper wells were dug to try and alleviate the problem. But years of pumping had taken their toll.

Gage abandoned his thoughts of his old hometown and came back to the present. He looked to the south and could see brownish-orange clouds of dust. His shift, which involved looking for problems and canal breaches, was seven hours that day, but he already felt tired at 3:00 p.m. His temperature gauge read 131°. As he swatted the last of the hoppers from his shirt, he pulled some greenish electrolyte drink from his pack and took two large swigs. Slightly refreshed, he followed the canal with his eyes east to where it disappeared from view into the brown mountain ranges.

JULY 23

DEER VALLEY

AIR TEMP 115°F, 6:00 A.M.

JACK MILLER HIT THE BRAKES hard on his Honda cycle. He squinted into the distance. He had been on patrol in Deer Valley all night, was rightly tired, and was about to go off shift.

He was near the edge of the CAP canal and thought he saw a man struggling in the canal, trying to swim. This wasn't unusual, since occasionally people who were drunk or high would fall into the canal. The lucky ones were rescued when some passersby saw them struggling.

Jack drove the bike closer and saw that the man was fairly close to the canal edge, bobbing up and down and swallowing water as he attempted to tread water.

Jack parked the bike, called in his location to dispatch and then called 911. He headed for the edge of the canal.

The guy went under several times. Jack tried to encourage him: "Hold on; help is coming."

Jack paused on the edge, and then, seeing that the man didn't have much strength left, decided to go in after him. He reached the man quickly, placed a lifesaving hold on him, and quickly swam to the side. However, the sides of the canals were slippery, and Jack struggled for a few minutes before getting them both onto the bank.

As they lay by the side of the canal, Jack checked the man out. He had on some worn clothes and cowboy boots and appeared to be about fifty. By the look and smell of him, Jack thought he was probably homeless.

"What happened to you, man?" Jack asked.

"I was walking by this canal and fell in."

His breath smelled of alcohol.

"Have you been drinking?"

"Hell no, officer. I don't drink!"

"OK, we need to get you to an emergency room. The EMTs are on the way."

As he spoke, the ambo drove up, the EMTs placed the man in the back, and they drove off to the nearest hospital.

JOHN C. LINCOLN NORTH HOSPITAL ER, DEER VALLEY

AIR TEMP 116°F, 8:30 A.M.

IT WAS 8:30 A.M. by the time the man was finally seen by the resident, Dr. DeShawn Otis, in the ER at John C. Lincoln North.

"You're lucky, my friend. You would have drowned if the cop hadn't seen you," Otis said.

"Yeah, whatever."

"We ran some labs on you. They're pretty much normal except for your sugar—very low. I guess you haven't eaten much in the last twenty-four hours. And your heart is skipping some beats. Could be AFib. By the way, did you hit your lip on the edge of the canal?"

"I don't know."

"Well, you had some bleeding from your lips and mouth when you came in."

"I guess I might have scraped it when the cop got me."

"In any case, we'd like to keep you. Watch you for a day or so."

"I don't have any insurance."

"Yeah, I figured that. But in Arizona, the state health plan will cover you."

"Whatever."

The man was left on his gurney and wheeled into the hall, a common practice in busy ERs. Sometimes they didn't have room for the volume of patients they were seeing, and John C. Lincoln, the major trauma center in North Phoenix, was no exception. The ER nurse wired him for an EKG, saw only a few extra beats, and then left to care for other patients.

JOHN C. LINCOLN ER, 11:00 A.M.

Dr. Otis heard the ambulance tech as the next patient came through the door, a man from Deer Valley who had woken up that morning, gone to work, and then had begun to cough up blood.

"Sixty-three-year-old male, hemoptysis, BP 95 systolic, pulse 119, respirations 25. Bringing up moderate amount of blood with cough for three hours, somewhat unstable," the EMT called out.

Otis went to examine the man. He heard some raspy sounds in his chest and then began to question him.

"Any history of coccidioidomycosis, also known as Valley Fever?'

"No."

"Are you on aspirin, anticoagulants? Any previous lung surgery, any COPD?"

"No," the man replied. "I think I'm in good health. Just a little overweight."

"I'm going to get a chest X-ray to check for pneumonia although you don't have a temp. I'll run some labs too. Then I'll be back"

Otis left the man in the care of his RN and went to check on another patient.

When the young doctor returned fifteen minutes later, the man had deteriorated. His blood pressure had dropped to 89/69. He now appeared listless and drowsy, and as Otis was about to check his lungs, he lost consciousness. A small pool of brownish fluid began to appear from his mouth, spreading out onto the lowest points of the pillow.

"Let's get some more fluid into him," Otis said to the nurse.

The chest X-ray had appeared normal, and the resident had seen none of the infiltrates that characterized pneumonia or other lung problems. And no patchy dots that sometimes accompanied Valley Fever. As Otis watched the RN hang another liter of fluid, the man's EKG suddenly flatlined, and in spite of the resuscitation team's best efforts, he died.

Another patient had come in while the resuscitation team was working. A sixty-seven-year-old female complained of shortness of breath and was coughing up a moderate amount of brownish fluid. All her tests came back negative, including her chest X-ray. She had no history of cocci. Within an hour she also deteriorated, and she expired at 1:00 p.m.

JOHN C. LINCOLN ER, 2:00 P.M.

Dr. Otis got beeped just as he was finishing a chest pain case.

"DeShawn, remember the homeless guy who came in this morning from the canal?" the RN asked.

"Yeah."

"He's bleeding out."

Otis ran into the hallway. He reached the side of the gurney and felt the man's carotid for a pulse, but there was nothing.

"How long's this guy been out?" he yelled.

"Don't know. After we read his EKG, he was left here to recover with a glucose drip," responded the nurse.

"That must have been five hours ago," Otis replied angrily.

Otis glanced at the man's face. A small rivulet of brownish-red fluid had spread itself under his head.

"Must be a stomach ulceration—probably alcohol," Otis said. DeShawn had seen a lot of these homeless addicts lately.

The resident quickly began CPR, gave the man some oxygen, epi, and multiple shocks, but his pulse never returned.

"Shit, this is what's going to happen if we leave people in the hall like this!"

"Probably," said the intern who had been assigned to him.

"You know, let's autopsy him," Otis said. "We need a new case for the ER M&M conference next week, and his stomach could be interesting."

"OK," replied the intern. "I'll set it up."

At the Morbidity and Mortality conference, the homeless man got more medical attention in death than he ever had in life. The pathology resident had prepared some heart, lung, and liver slides in addition to stomach slides. His stomach showed typical alcoholic ulcerations. Interestingly, one of the pathology residents noticed some lung alveolar swelling and partially destroyed cells in one of the lung slides. At the conference he presented the theory that the homeless man had also had a chronic Valley Fever infection.

The case was reported to the Arizona Department of Health Services, per state protocols.

JULY 23

NORTH CENTRAL
PHOENIX

AIR TEMP 132°F, 4:00 P.M.

CAITLYN AND BROOKLYN played together in the family pool. Their parents, Luca and Emma, had moved the family to Phoenix in 2027 from Toronto, Canada, in search of a warmer climate. The family had soon acclimated to the desert. Their two children attended a private school and were now ages seven and nine.

By the early 2030s, however, the couple realized that Phoenix was not the desert Eden they had initially thought it was. With the rising summertime temperatures and increasing dust storms, they occasionally thought of moving back to Canada, but Luca was too entrenched in his career as a luxury home developer for wealthy Arizonans. So, they continued to give their kids everything money could buy: new bikes, new clothes, the latest phones, expensive trips to see their grandparents in Italy, and anything else they wanted. Luca, as a developer dealing with wealthy clients, believed that he needed to maintain his image. He would treat himself to a new luxury car every few years. His latest was a Porsche X-700.

When it came time to upgrade their backyard pool, money was no object. They built a slide for the kids and two other water play stations. One looked like a dinosaur with a fountain coming out of its mouth, and the other was a new Jacuzzi just for the kids.

The sisters had been trying to dunk each other all afternoon. Brooklyn, being older and taller, would resist Caitlyn and dunk her instead. As a result, Caitlyn would get dunked many more times than Brooklyn. And when Caitlyn zoomed down the slide, she would often fall forward into the water.

After a while, Caitlyn became fed up with the dunking.

"Come on, Brooklyn. Let's go inside. I'm tired," Caitlyn begged.

"OK, but I won the dunking contest."

"Yeah, whatever. Just wait till next time," Caitlyn said.

They both climbed out of the pool and went inside to dry off.

"Girls, time for dinner," Emma called. "You can do your homework after dinner. Daddy and I are going out, so I'm turning on the Nanny Sitter this evening."

"Yeah, Mom," Brooklyn and Caitlyn answered.

The Nanny Sitter was a sophisticated robot that could be programmed to take care of children ages five to twelve. It resembled a large teddy bear, and the girls had gotten used to its mannerisms and voice. In fact, they had given it the nickname of "Bear." It was also programmed to set up Caitlyn's asthma nebulizer and perform many other medical maneuvers if necessary.

The family all sat down to dinner, made on the new stainless grill that Luca had recently purchased. After dinner, Caitlyn and Brooklyn went to their bedrooms to do their homework. At 7:00 p.m. Emma turned Bear on and programmed it for the evening. Bear replied with a gentle voice, "I will put them to bed at 9:00 p.m. Have a good night out." Shortly thereafter, Luca and Emma left for the evening.

About 9:30 p.m., the robot registered the sound of coughing from Caitlyn's room. It wasn't unusual for Caitlyn to cough. She had been diagnosed with childhood asthma, and her pediatrician had prescribed an inhaler and occasional steroids. But when the coughing turned to a raspy, croaky cough, the robot's programming kicked in, and it went to investigate.

"Caitlyn, what's going on?" Bear asked in a soothing voice.

"I don't feel good," came the reply. "I've got a tummy ache, and my cough is getting worse."

"OK, you must have another neb treatment."

The robot took Caitlyn out to the kitchen and set up the nebulizer machine for her. After ten minutes or so of the neb, her cough disappeared, and she was breathing better.

"OK, off to bed," Bear instructed, gently guiding the little girl back to her room.

As the robot returned to its post in the living room, it assessed the situation. Brooklyn was sound asleep. Luca and Emma were expected at midnight or later. The programming dropped down into power-save mode.

About 11:00 p.m., Bear registered an unusual noise in Caitlyn's room. As it glided to Caitlyn's door to investigate, it registered Caitlyn on the edge of her bed, rasping for air.

"I . . . I . . . can't breathe. Help! Help!"

The robot almost turned to get the nebulizer but then computed that Caitlyn's problem wasn't only the asthma. The robot's visual sensors registered that she was turning blue and was coughing up a bit of brownish, bloody fluid. Her voice thickened and then weakened as the coughing got worse. She was now gasping with every breath.

Suddenly, Caitlyn stopped coughing and fell over onto the bedroom floor.

As she hit the floor, she began gasping again, and there was a funny gurgling sound coming from her throat.

By this time, Brooklyn woke up from the commotion

and went to Caitlyn's room. She ran to her sister and started shaking her.

"Caitlyn! What's wrong?"

Brooklyn then looked up at the robot and yelled, "Bear, what's wrong with Caitlyn?"

"Unknown. Computing algorithms. Dialing 911," was the answer. The robot sitter was preprogrammed with Caitlyn's complete medical history and the latest health algorithms for her asthma and many other potential emergencies.

At that moment, the 911 call triggered another automatic notification algorithm for Bear to call Luca and Emma and to begin sending video and voice of the incident to the parents. Their phones beeped loudly with a special alarm. The video feed showed their daughter on the floor of her bedroom gasping for air. Luca and Emma ran to Luca's Porsche and began driving home.

The robot's medical programming took over as it searched for the cause of Caitlyn's symptoms.

"Caitlyn, do you have any pain in your tummy or chest?" Bear asked.

Barely able to speak, Caitlyn replied, "My chest, my chest. . . . It hurts."

Brooklyn felt very frightened by what was happening to her sister. Even though she had seen Caitlyn wheeze from the asthma many times before, she thought this seemed more serious and cried out, "Oh . . . Caitlyn . . . oh . . . what's that blood? Why are you shaking?"

Three minutes later, the EMTs arrived at the house.

"How long has this been going on?"

"Six minutes and 45 seconds," the robot replied. "She started coughing and then collapsed."

"OK, let's get her over to Scottsdale Shea Pediatric ER."

As the EMTs put an IV line in Caitlyn and put a breathing mask over her face, Brooklyn began screaming and crying.

"Where are Mommy and Daddy? Why don't they come home?"

As the EMTs sped away, Bear tried to comfort the sobbing girl. It computed that it hadn't updated Emma and Luca about Caitlyn, so it beeped their phones.

"Luca and Emma, EMTs have taken Caitlyn to Shea Pediatric ER. She started wheezing badly even after I nebbed her and was gasping for air."

"What?" Luca said. "What's happening, Bear?"

"Unknown," the robot replied.

Emma's face suddenly turned to terror.

"Let's go! Hurry!"

Luca reprogrammed the Porsche's GPS to Shea Pediatric ER. Emma was trembling. Caitlyn was her baby girl. Even though they had taken Caitlyn to the urgent care before for minor things, Emma couldn't help worrying that this might be something more serious.

As the ambo rolled into Shea Pediatric, one of the top three pediatric units in Phoenix, the head EMT called out the case to the Chief Resident: "Seven-year-old female, history of childhood asthma, on albuterol and nebs, wheezy, bloody cough since 11:00 p.m., BP 83/49, pulse 118 and thready, O2 is 79 percent. She's lost a lot of blood. Normal saline line running on the way."

Grabbing the gurney, the ER team quickly wheeled Caitlyn into the respiratory bay. The nurse put an IV into the girl's tibia bone for quicker access.

"Let's get a chest CT stat, and I want a CBC, bmp, lytes, and rapid cocci antibodies," the resident called out.

Caitlyn lay motionless on the gurney, slowly turning blue even with the oxygen mask on. It became obvious to the staff that she was in the fight of her life.

The nurse quickly placed a nanosensor on Caitlyn's chest, and the rapid labs came back in fifteen seconds showing a hemoglobin of 8.0 and hematocrit of 29 percent, both way below normal ranges. But the CT puzzled the Chief Resident.

"We've got some blood in both lower lobes, but no other pathology. How can that be? Get pulmonary down here. Stat!"

By now, Caitlyn's blood pressure had dropped dangerously low, and just then, her heart stopped beating.

As the pulmonary resident ran into the room, the Chief Resident called for a code. The team worked on the little girl for over ten minutes, but she couldn't be revived.

"Time of death, 12:13 a.m." noted the Chief Resident.

At that moment the Porsche squealed to a halt just outside the Shea ER, and Emma and Luca ran in. When they heard the news, Emma broke out into a loud sob and then a wail. Luca just stood there with a stunned look on his face.

"I'm really sorry," the Chief Resident said. "We did all we could. I don't know what happened. We're not sure where the bleeding was coming from."

Emma continued to wail and collapsed into Luca's arms.

"We're going to do an autopsy," the Chief Resident continued gently. "It's required for children in Arizona ERs. We should have results in a couple of days."

When Luca and Emma got home, they broke the news to Brooklyn. At first, Brooklyn didn't believe her parents, but then, as the reality sank in, she began sobbing uncontrollably. Emma tried to comfort her. Luca quietly turned off the nanny robot.

Two days later, they got a call from the Chief Resident who had cared for their daughter.

"Caitlyn's results are back. Her lungs showed signs of her asthma, some bleeding in both lower lobes, but no sign of tumors or other causes of the hemorrhaging. I'm sorry. That's all we know. Her other organs were entirely normal. By the way, we had another young girl that morning who was coughing blood. We thought it might be Valley Fever, but like your daughter, we just couldn't figure out what was happening. We were able to bronchoscope one of the girl's lungs and are looking into the pathology slides. I'll let you know if we find anything."

JULY 23

OLD TOWN SCOTTSDALE

AIR TEMP 132°F, 4:00 P.M.

"IT'S A BEAST," Noah said to his friend Jeremiah. Jeremiah stood there in the afternoon sun admiring Noah's new Ferrari 521. Noah proudly went around the car, showing off its many features, which included racing wheels, gull wing doors, and, of course, the best feature of all, four of the latest electric motors, with a combined horsepower of 425. Jeremiah sat himself down in the driver's seat.

"What's her 0 to 60 time?"

"2.9 seconds, Jere."

"Holy shit, dude! What's the pickup ratio?"

"Six girls to a block, if that's what you mean."

"I don't know how any babe could resist a ride in this!

Show me what she can do."

"OK, buddy!"

Fancy, souped-up cars regularly cruised the roads in north Scottsdale, and Ferraris were common. But at a $400,000 list price, only the wealthy few could afford one.

Noah floored the beast, and two girls on the corner by the shopping center turned to see the front of the car virtually jump off the pavement. Noah headed east to the 101, notorious for bottlenecks, and began weaving to and fro within the heavy traffic. A recent dust storm had made visibility subpar, and the sun would be setting soon.

They headed north on the highway, exceeding 145 mph briefly before Noah throttled back.

"Wow. Some acceleration!" Jeremiah exclaimed.

"Yeah, not bad."

Noah turned off the 101 and headed west toward the TPC Scottsdale golf course, where the Phoenix Open was held. He accelerated from 60 to 90 quickly, even though the limit there was 60. The road alongside the golf course was long and straight for two to three miles and Noah held his foot down on the accelerator. The car purred along: 90, 100, 110.

As they approached the end of the golf course, Jeremiah could see the whitish-brown sides of the CAP canal in the afternoon sun as the car approached the canal from the southeast.

"Hey, bud, shouldn't you slow down?"

"Nah, I'm only starting."

As the Ferrari closed on the canal, Noah saw two women on the sidewalk waving at him and gunned the motor.

"Look out!" Jeremiah screamed.

Noah hit the brakes, but they both felt a huge crunch, then a sensation of flying as the Ferrari hit the sloping bank of the canal and rocketed into the air like a missile. Jeremiah saw the white bank of the canal, heard the engines begin to whine down, saw the blue of the sky, and then briefly felt the sensation of weightlessness as the arc of the car approached its zenith.

It seemed like time was suspended as the car hung in midair. Jeremiah thought about his wife and kids, and part of his life flashed before him. Soon the Ferrari began descending, and with a loud splash the car hit the middle of the canal. With the four heavy electric motors, the Ferrari started sinking rapidly into the water.

Jeremiah was able to open his door and get out of the car quickly, but Noah had trouble releasing his buckle, and the car began to sink below the water level. Noah started crying out for help as the water level rose. Jeremiah at first could only watch as Noah's head went under.

Jeremiah was initially dazed by the accident, but then the water awakened him. He dived under and after about twenty seconds was able to open Noah's door and get him out. By that time, Noah had swallowed a lot of water and was gasping for air.

The two women on the street had gotten out their cell

phones and had made the emergency call to 911.

Noah was semiconscious as Jeremiah attempted to get him to the side of the canal. He remembered his Red Cross rescuer training and eventually was able to get Noah onto the canal edge, which was quite steep. By that time, the ambulance had arrived, and two EMTs helped get Noah and then Jeremiah out of the water.

"I think he swallowed a lot of water," Jeremiah said. "We hit the canal pretty hard."

"Yeah, looks like it," one of the EMTs responded as they began CPR on Noah, who had lost consciousness.

"How long was he down in the water?"

"I think almost a minute," Jeremiah replied.

The EMTs continued CPR for about two minutes, and then Noah came to, spurting water from his mouth. They gave him oxygen, checked his vitals, got him in the ambulance, and prepared to head to the nearest ER, which was Scottsdale Mayo.

"Can I go along? He's my best friend, and I want to make sure he's OK," Jeremiah said. He could barely believe what had happened. He was visibly shaken by Noah's appearance, which wasn't good. Noah had several deep cuts on his face, and one of his ankles was swollen. That foot jutted out at a funny angle.

"OK, climb aboard."

The trip to Mayo was a quick three minutes, and they were there before Jeremiah knew it. The EMTs burst through the ER doors.

"Male, thirty-two, car crash in the canal, a large amount of water imbibed," said one. "Unconscious in the water for one minute, resuscitated on the canal bank. Vitals are BP 145 systolic, p O2 86 percent, pulse 105."

The Mayo Clinic had come to the Valley in the late 1990s and was respected as one of the top two medical institutions in Phoenix. As Noah was placed on a gurney and taken to a room, the Chief Resident, Dr. Julio Morales, asked Jeremiah, "Do you know his medical history?"

"Yeah. He likes to have a few. I know that. Other than that, no. He doesn't tell me much about his doctor visits. He has a girlfriend in Scottsdale."

"OK, thanks."

Julio approached Noah's bed, where Noah had woken up. The doc quickly examined him, focusing on his neck, head, and major joints.

"Any pain here?" Julio asked as he poked on Noah's ribs, neck, and back.

"Ow, that really hurts!" Noah cried as the resident pressed on his knee and ankle area.

"I'm going to get some leg and ankle films. Do you have any major medical problems? Taking any meds?"

"I've been hitting the booze pretty hard. A lot of partying in Scottsdale for a few years. My primary doc said I probably have some liver issues by now," Noah admitted.

"OK, let's get liver enzymes, a CBC, basic metabolic panel, hepatitis panel, clotting panels, cocci antibodies," Julio instructed the robot nurse standing by.

"Your vitals have stabilized, so I'll be back when the labs come in. You're damn lucky you didn't meet the reaper today. The police said you hit the canal bank at about a hundred! And your friend saved you. You were under water for at least a minute."

"I know," Noah said with a garbled voice as he looked over at Jeremiah. "He's my best buddy."

Jeremiah took a chair by his friend's bedside as the robot nurse drew Noah's blood.

"Hold still now. It won't hurt much," said a soothing female voice.

After about ten minutes, Dr. Morales appeared, drew the curtains back, and approached Noah, who had dozed off from the trauma of the accident.

"Looks like you were right. Your liver enzymes are all fouled up. AST is off the charts at 1400. ALT is 990 and your PT and PTT are huge! How much are you drinking per week, my man?"

"Oh, maybe five or six hard shots four or five times a week. And on the weekends, more."

"Hmmm. By the way, you also have a pretty severe lateral ankle fracture. I'm going to call ortho, and they'll probably want to cast you after we get the swelling down. So we're going to keep you for a day or two. We may want to do a liver biopsy, but we can do that later. For now, we want you to get some rest, and we're going to watch your liver function closely. Do you want us to call your girlfriend?"

"Yeah, I guess. That would be nice. Her name's Kennedy. Jeremiah can give you her number."

The resident took Kennedy's number, gave instructions to the robot nurse to call her, spoke orders into his tablet for Noah to be admitted to the ortho floor, and then went off to see other patients.

It was 9:00 p.m. before Noah was put in a bed on the fourth floor. Jeremiah had stayed by his friend's side until he went up to his room. They said goodbye for the night. The robot nurse had been unable to reach Noah's girlfriend, and after the ortho resident on call had splinted Noah's ankle, he had fallen off to sleep. He had an IV for fluids, and a single nanomonitor placed on the skin near his heart recorded his heart pattern, blood pressure, O2 Sats, pulse, electrolytes, and even some clotting parameters.

In days past, multiple monitors were needed to record these parameters, but in 2036 this single nanomonitor, about 1/16 inch in diameter, did all the work. In addition, a small wall camera kept a close eye on the patient. A central computer, fed by the nanomonitors, kept track of all the patients in the hospital. If a problem arose, an on-call team of hospitalists was available to treat whatever came up. The computer was programmed for all known scenarios and had a 99.95 percent accuracy rate for clinical diagnostics.

At 4:32 a.m., the camera in Noah's room recorded an unusual event. While Noah was in second-stage REM sleep, the camera observed a small amount of brownish mucus leave Noah's mouth and stain his pillow.

The computer immediately checked his clotting parameters. They were unchanged since admission. It cross-checked his medical history and noted his liver disease.

At 4:35 a.m., Noah began to cough slightly while he slept, and the camera recorded a slight discharge of brownish blood from Noah's nose.

At 4:36 a.m., the computer recorded a sudden drop in Noah's blood pressure, from 131/84 to 118/71. This triggered the computer to send an alarm notice to the hospitalists, who were just finishing a video game in the cafeteria.

JULY 24

MAYO SCOTTSDALE
EMPLOYEE CAFETERIA

4:36 A.M.

ERIC HAD WORKED for Mayo as a hospitalist for three years and enjoyed the regular hours and excellent pay. His new wife, Brittany, liked his hours too since they meshed with her hours as a night shift RN. As Eric made his way to Noah's room, he had already been briefed by the central computer about Noah's case. Eric had worked out the likely cause of Noah's bleeding, which was certainly the liver disease and messed-up clotting parameters. He had reviewed the labs for coccidioidomycosis, and the cocci antibodies were negative.

Eric knew that the Valley metro area was in the throes of a cocci epidemic, and bloody cough could be one of the symptoms of this common illness, especially with the recent increase in dust storms. However, the labs had ruled that out.

As he reached the elevator to Noah's section, Eric received an ominous warning from the central computer through his virtual glasses: "Parameters dropping, heart rate increasing, BP dropping rapidly."

Once off the elevator, Eric ran into Noah's room just in time to see Noah cough and vomit a large gob of mucus-laden blood and then suddenly start convulsing uncontrollably.

The central computer came back on immediately and stated, "BP 84/56, pulse 135, heartbeat erratic and decaying."

Eric checked Noah for a pulse, then began CPR. At the same time, he called a code into his virtual set, "Room 443, code team stat!"

Each hospital had a code team that was expertly trained in the latest resuscitation techniques. In a large hospital such as Mayo, the teams might be used up to twenty-five times a day. This saved the hospital from relying on the weak skills of newly minted interns and residents. Having these trained teams had increased the code recoveries from 10 percent to 34 percent in just one year.

The team arrived in twelve seconds and began its work. Eric continued to help with the CPR. In another twenty-five seconds, a line was placed, and meds were given. But everyone in the room could see this would be an unlikely recovery. With the coags off, even if they could get

Noah's heart up again, he would likely continue to bleed.

After ten minutes they called it. The lead member of the code team said, "Time of death 4:48 a.m."

"Time of death 4:48 a.m.," the central computer repeated.

Eric notified the ortho resident in charge about Noah's death and headed back to the cafeteria. The resuscitation attempts were tiring, even though it had become a commonplace occurrence since the hospitals now admitted only the sickest patients. Noah had been the fifth resuscitation attempt on his shift that day, and he was emotionally drained.

Dr. Morales ordered an autopsy along with sections of Noah's liver, heart, and lungs. Two days later, he was viewing the slides with a new pathology intern.

"See the liver cells," he said. "They appear larger than usual, and see all the lymphocytes surrounding them? Indication of inflammation. Common for alcoholic liver cirrhosis. The bile duct is inflamed, too."

As Morales scanned the lung and alveolar slides under high magnification, something caught his eye. In a normal lung slide, the one-cell-thick lining of the alveolus would be regular, with the cells lining up next to one another like little blocks. The cells would be pretty much the same size. This allowed for the easy exchange of oxygen into the bloodstream and the release of carbon dioxide out through the breath. But he noticed that a lot of Noah's alveolar cells had broken down and thus appeared in different, irregular sizes. And there was another thing. Normally, the tiny arterioles and veinules that supplied the alveoli had a regular lining, much like the alveolar lining. But as he looked closer under the highest optical magnification, 7000x, he could see that the blood vessel cells surrounding the alveolus appeared highly abnormal, with little clumps of cell walls here and there. Normally, these cell walls would appear intact and regular, much like the alveolar cells.

"Huh, maybe from the water in his lungs, but I really can't explain this," he told the intern shadowing him. He filed the slides away for future study.

MAYO ER ROOM 1, 7:00 A.M.

"Sixty-five-year-old male, history of cocci exposure, BP 100/68, pulse 118, pO2 84, presenting with a bad cough," the EMTs called out as they quickly wheeled the man into the building.

"You'd better get a line in," the resident called to a nurse.

"Copy that," he replied.

"So, he's seen a lot of cocci?" the resident asked.

"Yeah, apparently he was outside in numerous dust storms lately. Works as an APS lineman."

MAYO ER ROOM 2, 8:15 A.M.

"Forty-eight-year-old female, history of gastric ulcer, BP 87/60, pulse 126, pO2 90."

"Stewart, get a line in this one stat. And send for CBC, BMP and coags."

"Will do," the RN replied.

"Any cocci history?"

"Maybe."

"OK, get cocci antibodies too," the resident added.

MAYO ER ROOM 3, 9:31 A.M.

"Another bleeder?" the resident asked the EMTs.

"Yeah, 59-year-old male, history of bad COPD and cocci exposure."

"He looks terrible."

"PO2 was only 80, so we've got him on 100 percent oxygen, but 80 is all we can get to. He's a meter reader for APS and was outside a lot in some dust storms."

"OK, get cocci antibodies, cocci antigen, CBC, and coags. We've had a lot of these cocci exposures lately."

A robot approached the man. A small mechanical arm extended and carefully pushed a blood needle into the man's antecubital vein.

MAYO ER ROOM 4, 10:07 A.M.

"Get this guy some blood," the EMTs yelled as they wheeled the gurney through the door. "He's got a history of alcoholic liver disease and cocci exposure also. When we picked him up, he was unconscious, and the BP was only 86/54. Current O2 is only 79. A bad one. We had to resuscitate him twice on the way in."

"OK, get a line in and hang two liters of normal saline stat. Then get a CBC, BMP, cocci antibodies, liver panel, and coags."

The phlebotomy robot complied, and one hundred seconds later, the labs came back: liver enzymes over twelve hundred, hemoglobin low at 8.8, and positive for cocci.

MAYO EMPLOYEE CAFETERIA, 12:30 P.M.

The new ER residents looked at each other.

"Been here only two weeks now, and this cocci stuff is getting worse," said one.

"Yeah," the other resident replied. "I agree. I've even seen some deaths from the cocci. Once their lungs are compromised, they can't stop coughing. Sometimes they break a lung vessel and bleed out or develop terminal pneumonia."

"Saw three or four of those just this morning."

"Really. I've seen a bunch today also. All ages. Usually comorbidities along with the cocci."

"Yeah, and the Chief has ordered us to collect sputum swabs and do posts on all patients that expire from the cocci. It's under a new public health order from Dr. Weiss over at the state public health office after the start of the dust storms a few days ago. They want to see if the cocci strains are the same as in last year's outbreak. We'll send them the cocci patients' sputum for DNA sequencing."

The two residents headed back to the ER. Over the course of the afternoon, they treated twenty-four suspected cases of coccidioidomycosis exposure, with nineteen deaths. But there were twelve deaths that couldn't be explained by the cocci.

When they got off shift at 6:00 p.m. that evening, a virtual TV in the ER waiting room was blaring, "Breaking News! Twelve unexplained deaths today at Mayo Scottsdale. ER doctors are puzzled since the deaths aren't from the recent cocci outbreak."

The station switched to a video of Dr. Weiss being interviewed by a reporter for 5News.

"Yes, we have some unexplained cases."

"Could this be a new virus like MERS or another coronavirus?" the reporter asked.

"Well, we just don't know at this time," Dr. Weiss replied.

JULY 24

PHYSICIAN'S LOUNGE, SCOTTSDALE OSBORN MEDICAL CENTER

AIR TEMP 130°F, 1:23 P.M.

"HEY, DID YOU HEAR about that rush of Valley Fever cases this morning at Mayo?" Ethan Mason, a second-year resident in emergency medicine, asked his buddy Tim Gonzales.

"No, how many?" Tim replied.

Tim was a first-year ER resident and was enjoying the experience he was getting in the Honor Health system.

"Twenty-four in one shift."

"Holy shit!"

"Yeah," Ethan said. "I put on an N95 mask every time we get a bad dust storm, and even then I sometimes cough for a whole day. I know we all have antibodies to cocci. History tells us that the worst cases are those with comorbidities, like asthma, COPD, or immune diseases, but lately, we're seeing patients without those comorbidities get really sick."

"I know," Tim said. "My sister got really sick with cocci last year and was in the hospital for three weeks."

"Is she OK now?"

"Yeah, but she has to be careful in the winter. Her lungs just aren't the same."

At that moment, a weather update came over the hospital computer system: "Dust update: Phoenix weather has recorded a large outbreak of dust with wind velocity approaching 55 mph fifteen miles south of the city, approaching rapidly. Southeast sectors expected to receive dust over the next twenty minutes. Air temperature approaching 135°F. Please take emergency precautions, including air filters. Maximum outdoor time allowed is seven minutes without a cooling vest. Dusk masks mandatory."

The loudspeaker clicked off.

Ethan and Tim looked at each other. They had only been on shift for few hours, but the warning was ominous and probably meant they would see a lot more respiratory cases that afternoon. They took another minute to finish their coffee and then headed back to the ER.

Tim was called quickly to see a fifty-three-year-old male with severe chest pains. Ethan was evaluating a young girl with a wrist fracture when the doors blew open and two ambo teams wheeled gurneys in. One held a sixty-three-year-old female who was coughing badly and bringing up brownish mucus with each cough. On the other gurney a seventy-seven-year-old male lay motionless, with blood oozing from his mouth and nose.

They each took one patient—Tim the man and Ethan the woman.

"We almost didn't make it here," one EMT said. "Almost no visibility and gusts must have been up near 50."

Ethan and Tim were trying to question the two patients when two other ambo teams hit the ER.

"Forty-nine-year-old male with history of COPD, O2 at 81, picked him up in the dust storm."

"Eight-year-old female, no significant history, found unconscious by her parents this morning in her bed. Upon transfer found to be bleeding profusely from the mouth. No history of cocci exposure past or recent. No other medical problems."

The girl's case caused Ethan to pause. Every other patient that morning had had dust exposure, and with the storm on top of them, they expected these types of patients. But an eight-year-old healthy girl?

"What's her oxygen Sat and vitals?" he asked the EMT team.

"Sat is 79. BP 74/49 and falling. Pulse 128. Respirations 26 and labored."

"Get a bone line in her," Ethan said. "And I want a CBC, BMP, coags, cocci antigen, cocci antibodies, chest

CT. And call pulmonary. Stat!"

As Ethan waited for the pulmonologist on call, he examined the little girl. He saw the blood oozing from her mouth but noticed no marks of trauma. He placed a 100 percent O2 mask over her face and waited about thirty seconds for her O2 Sat to improve, but it kept dropping. The pulmonologist arrived as he finished checking her Sat.

Just then, the parents ran in.

"Doctor, what's happening?" the mother asked.

Dr. Winter, the pulmonary specialist, had seen a lot of kids recently with cocci. She was surprised to see this girl without a cocci history in her present state.

"Any recent dust or cocci exposure?" Winter asked the parents.

"No, and she definitely has been inside for the last four or five days. We were worried about the air quality."

"Huh. And no history of asthma or hemophilia?"

"No, totally healthy."

She quickly examined the girl after they had placed the line and given her oxygen. Her chest, particularly the right side, was full of deep-sounding, raspy rhonchi, usually a sign of infection.

"Her temp is normal?"

"Yes, 98.8," the nurse said.

"OK, I want to bronch her. I know it's risky, but unless we get to the cause of her bloody cough, I don't think she has a chance."

A robot appeared almost instantaneously with the bronchoscopy gear, and the RN prepped the little girl for the procedure. By now, she appeared totally pale. Winter began the procedure as the robot escorted the parents out of the room.

"I don't see anything in the posterior pharynx. The upper trachea is totally normal, blood's coming from lower down." Winter said. "I'm at the carina; there's a lot of blood and mucus here. Going into the left bronchus. A little bleeding and oozing, but not enough to explain what's coming from her mouth.

"Retracting and entering the right bronchus. . . . Holy shit! There's bright red blood everywhere—possibly from deep in the bronchioles. Can't find the bleeding source, don't see a mass, tumor, or AV malformation here."

At that moment, the tiny biosensor chip that had been placed on the girl's chest gave a loud warning: "BP dropping rapidly, pulse diminishing, O2 dropping."

The pulmonologist quickly retracted the bronchoscope as the code team rushed in and began to pump the little girl's chest.

After nine minutes the central computer called out, "Expiration at 2:32 p.m."

The entire team was dejected to lose such a young patient.

"I'm going to call for an autopsy," Winter said, looking extremely puzzled and upset. "I can't explain this. Get the parents in here, and I'll tell them. If they don't

209

object, I want to see all of the path slides."

Ethan heard about the little girl's passing as he and Tim spent the rest of the afternoon taking care of multiple cases of cocci exposure from the dust storm and several other cases of bronchial bleeds they couldn't explain. As per Scottsdale Osborn and state health department protocol, and with next-of-kin approval, the unexplained cases were autopsied, and multiple slides were taken from the major organ systems.

At 7:00 p.m., as Ethan was leaving the hospital at the end of his shift, he noticed a TV van from Phoenix Channel 3 come to a screeching halt outside the ER. A young female reporter ran up to him and began to throw questions: "We've heard about some more unexplained deaths. Can you comment on these cases, Dr. . . ."

"Dr. Mason," Ethan answered.

A small group of passersby began to gather around Ethan and the reporter, some beginning to anxiously yell, "What is this? Do you know what this could be? Is it another COVID?"

Ethan didn't have an immediate answer for the reporter, but as the crowd began to grow, he extricated himself from the questions. As he ran to his car, he could hear the reporter speak into her microphone,

"We have no definitive answer from an ER doc at Scottsdale Osborn, but today at 6:00 p.m., state public health placed investigators with infrared temperature detectors at Phoenix Sky Harbor International Airport to screen for unexpected cases. There were twelve unexplained deaths today at Mayo, several more today at Scottsdale Osborn, and thirty late today at Chandler Regional freestanding ER."

BANNER DENVER WEST, RESEARCH DIVISION

AIR TEMP 116°F, 9:00 P.M.

JEREMY STONE ORDERED a decaf mocha from the Starbucks robot and turned on the newsfeed in the clinical research area while he waited for his coffee. So far, everything was going well. The commotion and panic he saw reported on the news from Phoenix seemed far away. Even so, as a medical scientist, it mildly intrigued him that no cause had been found for the strange deaths in Arizona. He knew that Valley Fever was a major cause of desert pulmonary infections, so that, along with the possibility of a new SARS-like disease caused by a coronavirus, seemed to be the likely explanation. In any case, he was completely focused on his trials, so he gave no more thought to what was happening in Phoenix.

JULY 24

HARVARD SCHOOL OF PUBLIC HEALTH, BOSTON

AIR TEMP 94°F, 11:00 P.M.

JACOB MICHAELS, DPH, was watching a feed on national news. Michaels had returned from South Africa at the end of May, having conducted a successful operation against the latest Ebola outbreak in that country. He was an experienced epidemiologist, and the TV feed caught his attention immediately. He watched as panicked citizens in Phoenix gathered around a reporter at one of the hospitals, asking questions about what appeared to be an outbreak of an unknown organism.

Wonder what that's all about? he thought to himself.

JULY 25

STATE HEALTH DEPARTMENT, PHOENIX

AIR TEMP 115°F, 9:00 A.M.

RACHAEL WEISS, MD, DPH, was chief public health officer at the Arizona Department of Health Services and responsible for ensuring that all Arizona public health research and projects were completed on time. She oversaw nine departments with 1,700 employees, of which sixty were laboratory specialists.

Her budget for 2036 had been capped at $95 million by the legislature, which was about 15 percent less than usual. But a recent STD uptick and increase in cocci cases would require some additional funding.

Two weeks earlier, she had been busy following up on reports that Phoenix and some rural Arizona counties had been experiencing a significant increase of syphilis cases. However, in the last few days, she had become increasingly alarmed as reports of unexplained respiratory deaths began to issue from several ERs in the Valley metro area during and after two recent dust storms.

Dr. Weiss had spent the last fifteen years at the Arizona Department of Health Services, having trained at the Bloomberg School of Public Health at Johns Hopkins, obtaining her Doctor of Public Health degree in 2019. She had worked briefly for the health department in Houston before coming to Phoenix. Weiss was in her early forties. She had several close friends in the Phoenix area and back East, but because her work demanded much of her time, she had never married.

In Phoenix, she often worked closely with Deisy Munoz, MD, MPH, the federal public health officer in charge of the Arizona region and, specifically, the Phoenix area. Like Dr. Weiss, Dr. Munoz had trained on the East Coast at Boston University. After Boston, Munoz had been sent to Davis-Monthan Air Force Base in Tucson and then Luke Air Force Base near Phoenix to pay the Air Force back for her years of residency training. On this morning, the two sat in Dr. Weiss's office on the sixth floor of the state health building discussing the recent cases from the ERs.

"Rachael, have you learned anything about the cocci strains that are showing up in Phoenix?"

"No, not yet. We're taking samples from ERs after those bad dust storms on July 23 and July 24. We know, though, that cocci is increasing with the change in the climate. We hope to get enough samples to send to the sequencing lab here so we can see what we're up against. The docs in the ERs tell me that the recent cases have been much more difficult to treat.

"I'm going down to Tucson next week to talk with Dr. Corsini, who's head of the cocci research lab there, to see if he's got any new information. When I talked to the ER docs yesterday at Mayo, Scottsdale Osborn, and eight other ERs, they indicated that on July 23 and July 24, right in the middle of the dust storms, they saw a total of eight hundred cases of severe respiratory distress. Four hundred presented with hemoptyses that were cocci antibody negative. Out of those four hundred cases, nearly three hundred died in the ER, mostly from bleeding out. And I'm talking cases from about ten ERs over those dates, so about fifteen cases a day in each ER that can't be explained!

"The public is beginning to panic, the governor's asking for answers, and I've already been interviewed by two news stations in town, with more reporters clamoring for interviews. The clinical presentations just don't match anything that we're familiar with. At first, we thought it might be another coronavirus or new infection brought back from overseas, but none of the lab results match any such scenarios.

"I've placed some investigators at the airport to see if we can pinpoint any travelers who might be carrying new infections. They're using infrared forehead temperature sensors and quick diagnostic labs. But I have to tell you, when three hundred patients die for no known reason, and after the years with recurring COVID pandemics, people begin to panic.

"I'm sending Sandy Morrison, one of our MPH interns, out to a few of the ERs to investigate further."

"Sounds good. Let me know if you need any help," Deisy offered.

"OK, I appreciate that."

JULY 25

PHOENIX
METRO AREA

AIR TEMP 116°F, 9:30 A.M.

SANDY MORRISON MADE her way out of the downtown public health office later that morning. The wind was building from the south, and it looked like another dust day. She could see a large brownish-yellow cloud of dust moving toward the city. It seemed enormous and extended up into some low-hanging clouds.

Sandy was determined to finish her public health internship. Under the direction of Dr. Weiss, she had already learned a great deal, and having this cocci investigation on her résumé could prove invaluable in the future.

She hopped on the 101, exited at Tatum Boulevard, pulled into the ER lot at Mayo, and parked the Super Toyota. Just as she exited the car, the dust picked up, so she took care to put on her dust mask. Once in the ER, she spoke to the charge nurse, Melissa Chamberlain.

"Hi, I'm Sandy Morrison from the department of public health."

"I know. Dr. Weiss told me you would be coming," Chamberlain said. "Something about the July 24 patients seen in the ER for cocci?"

"Yes, and apparently there were some cases that couldn't be explained by the fungus. I'd like to speak personally with the residents who worked with these patients on that day."

"Let's see. I believe Dr. Nascha is here today."

"Great. Thanks."

Sandy took a seat in the nurse's office.

About five minutes later, Dr. Nascha appeared, and the two women introduced themselves.

"I understand you want some information on patients I saw on July 24."

"Yes. I'm an MPH intern at the office of public health. Tell me whatever you can about the patients that day."

"Sure. Dr. Kimball and I saw the bulk of the new patients that day. Kimball's off today, by the way. I believe, if I remember correctly, that we saw at least twenty-four respiratory patients, some with hemoptysis. But there was something weird about some of those patients."

"What's that?"

"Well, as you probably know, cocci can take days

or weeks for the body to produce antibodies detected in blood, but nowadays we can measure exposure antibodies to the fungus with real-time PCR, even though they've only been exposed for about twenty-four to forty-eight hours. We found the cocci easily in about twelve patients. But in the other twelve, no sign of any cocci. And there was something else."

Sandy leaned closer to the resident to listen.

"Most of the cocci–negative patients expired in the ER that day due to excessive bleeding. Normally with cocci, you don't see that kind of pulmonary bleeding, at least that early in the course of the disease," Nascha said.

"So, what do you think might have caused those deaths?"

"I'm not sure. Could be a new hemorrhagic virus or another novel coronavirus. But I'm just not sure."

"OK, I know you're busy. Do you have the slides from path and the nasal or sputum swabs?"

"We have slides on about twenty-two out of the twenty-four. The other two seem to have been lost."

"OK, that works."

Nascha left to obtain the slides from path and returned in about fifteen minutes.

"Here they are. They're already checked out via sign-off to Dr. Weiss, but they need to be returned within ten days."

"No problem. And thanks for your time."

"You're welcome. And let me know if you find

anything."

"Will do."

Sandy picked up the slide kit and samples and headed back to her car. She also grabbed a new level-three dust mask from the secretary on her way out.

By now the sky was filled with brown dust. As she climbed into the Super Toyota, she glanced at the outside temp—120 degrees at 11:00 a.m.

Jeez. Another hot one, she thought.

Sandy was from Flagstaff's higher elevation and still wasn't used to Phoenix temperatures. But this was summer in the Valley, and recent temps in the summer season were averaging 30–40 degrees higher than the high country.

Sandy drove down the 101 and then across the 60 into north Gilbert to visit the Dignity Health freestanding ER. She hoped to find some of the docs who had treated respiratory patients on July 24, the day of one of the biggest dust storms in Phoenix history.

The Valley metro area had been getting these storms for many years. At first, they were small and something of a curiosity, both for Valley residents and visitors. But in more recent years, they had become deadly. Vehicle crashes had escalated due to the decreased visibility. Planes often had to divert to other cities, and the worst problem was the increasing incidence of Valley Fever. This was the problem Sandy was studying for her master's thesis. And she hoped to get a lot of data to help with that.

She pulled into the parking lot in front of the Dignity Health freestanding ER. Several patients were being brought in by ambulance. Some were already coughing from the dust. Sandy put on her mask and went inside.

"Hi. Can you direct me to the administrator in charge?"

"Sure. Just a minute."

As she waited, she glanced down the long row of bays in the ER. There must have been at least fifteen or twenty of them. And this morning, about half of them were full of coughing patients.

"Hi, I'm Jenna Hathale, the ER administrator. I understand you're from public health. How can I help you?"

"Yes, I want to talk to the docs who were on duty on July 24, the day of the huge dust storm."

"July 24," Hathale said. She paused. "OK, yeah. . . . I remember that day well. What a horrible storm, and our ER was filled to capacity with respiratory cases. I think we had two locum tenens ER docs that day, Spencer Harris and Raquel Sabatino. Spencer was from Salt Lake, I believe, and I know Raquel came to us from LA. But you know, they went home yesterday."

"Is there any way to get ahold of them?" Sandy asked.

"Well, let's see. If you call CompHealth, they might be able to trace them, at least give you their home phone numbers or tell you if they've gone on to another fill-in assignment. In any case, let me get you the CompHealth number."

The administrator went back to her office and returned in a few minutes.

She handed Sandy a card with the phone number for CompHealth Salt Lake City.

"Awesome. I'll call them. By the way, Dr. Weiss is also requesting the path, autopsy reports, and swabs on the sixty respiratory patients that came in that day."

"No problem. Just a minute."

Hathale returned with the slide kits, swabs, and copies of the autopsy reports.

"Protocol states that these are to be loaned for no more than seven days."

"Yup, no worries."

"And let me know what you find. I was on duty that day, and I remember the docs were pretty puzzled by what they were seeing . . . all that blood."

"Will do."

Sandy got back into the Super Toyota. Cruising down the 60, she told the onboard computer to call CompHealth to get Harris's and Sabatino's cell numbers. She left a voice mail for Sabatino and was able to reach Harris directly. In a ten-minute conversation, he recalled the events of July 24.

"Yeah, busy day. I've never seen anything like it. We were overwhelmed by the sixty respiratory patients. I've seen a lot of respiratory patients and cocci patients in my time, but those thirty that we tried to resuscitate . . . I don't know . . . just something strange about them."

"What?" Sandy asked.

"Well, during the shift I had so much blood on my lab coat—I had to change it twice. Never seen so much hemoptysis in cocci patients. Usually only a small percentage are bringing up blood with their mucus."

"OK. Thanks for your help. Good to know," Sandy replied.

JULY 25

DR. WEISS'S OFFICE, STATE HEALTH DEPARTMENT

AIR TEMP 126F, 1:00 P.M.

WHEN SANDY RETURNED to the department of health building, Dr. Weiss was waiting for her. Sandy began her report.

"I managed to talk to Dr. Nascha, a resident at Mayo, and then the administrator at Dignity Health. The two locum docs that were at Dignity on the twenty-fourth had already left for other assignments, but I was able to reach one by phone on the way back here.

"They were all overwhelmed that day with cocci patients, especially after that huge dust storm on the twenty-fourth."

"Were the cocci presentations typical?" Weiss asked. "And did you get sputum or nasal swabs for the DNA lab here?"

"Yeah, the cocci patients seemed typical. The two ERs gave me swabs on thirty or so of the cocci patients, and there are forty swabs from the other cocci-negative patients that presented with severe hemoptysis."

"Good. I'm hoping we'll get some good DNA data from our lab—we've also got DNA data from last year's cocci epidemic to use as a comparison. Maybe you want to get involved?" Weiss offered. "It could mean your name on a paper, and that's always helpful."

"Awesome. Sounds great!" Sandy responded.

Sandy went off to take the samples downstairs to the DNA lab.

Meanwhile, Dr. Weiss rechecked the previous data on the patients. She activated a virtual screen that displayed cases and numbers as she called them out:

July 23–24, ten ERs in Phoenix reported eight hundred total acute respiratory patients.

Four hundred tested positive for cocci, and four hundred were cocci-free.

Seventy-five percent, or 300, of the cocci-free patients died from unknown causes.

As Weiss looked at the screen, her office computer spoke. She was used to getting real-time alerts from all over the world: "Urgent notice. London: British Health Service Alert. Dateline: July 25, 2036, Phoenix, Arizona, United States of America. Unknown organism suspected in respiratory outbreak with three hundred deaths in Phoenix metro area. Arizona travel restrictions in effect: Any travelers arriving from Phoenix must report to London health authorities at Heathrow and Gatwick Airports."

Holy shit! Weiss thought. We're already on the global stage!

She returned to the task at hand. Weiss had been forced to multitask due to staffing reductions from the recent budget cuts. The new epidemic of unexplained respiratory hemoptysis cases worried her more than intrigued her. But over her career, she had always been up for new challenges and had indeed solved some unwieldy problems. This would prove to be one of the most difficult.

DR. WEISS'S OFFICE, 4:00 P.M.

In the early days of DNA testing, it took nearly seven days to process a large amount of DNA on the old sequencers. But in the era of super high-speed computers connected to sequencers, twenty million base pairs of DNA could be sequenced in just under an hour.

At 4:00 p.m. the sample reports from the state lab were delivered to Dr. Weiss. She activated the virtual screen and called Sandy to come and review the data with her.

DNA SAMPLES #1-400: COCCI-POSITIVE PATIENTS FROM ERS 7/23-7/24

LAST YEAR'S (2035) COCCI STRAIN	= 396	(99%)
NEW MUTATION	= 4	(01%)

DNA SAMPLES #401-800: COCCI-NEGATIVE PATIENTS FROM ERS 7/23-7/24

NONCOCCI RESPIRATORY ILLNESS	= 100	(25%)
UNKNOWN ORGANISM	= 300	(75%)

NO ALIGNMENT FOUND IN NIH DATABASE: ORGANISM UNKNOWN

Alignment reflected the degree of correspondence between a known organism's sequence and the sample's sequence. The NIH maintained a current database of the DNA base pair sequences of all known organisms: bacteria, viruses, parasites, insects, animals, humans. Normally, lab samples could be matched to the DNA database in four seconds.

Rachael was incredulous.

"An unknown organism? What the hell? It looks like the cocci patients had a tiny portion of new mutations, but 75 percent of the 400 cocci-negative patients tested negative for any known organism! What could be causing this?"

She continued, "In 300 out of the four hundred patients, no alignments matched on the NIH database from all the known organisms in the entire world. That means that whatever we're dealing with is something totally new in nature."

Sandy chimed in.

"What about some new parasite or novel coronavirus?"

"That's always a possibility," Rachael said. "Still, it's very puzzling. It could be a new virus or virus-like organism. They had that new coronavirus outbreak this year in Thailand that Dr. Munoz told me about. Maybe a traveler came back to Phoenix and spread it by coughing. But that should have at least partially matched with known coronaviruses in the database."

Rachael considered for a moment and then said, "Let's take a walk down to microscopy and look at some slides."

STATE HEALTH DEPARTMENT, MICROSCOPY SUITE, PHOENIX, 4:30 P.M.

The microscopy suite on the second floor of the public health building boasted a new Zeiss Confocal 7000 scope. The scope had been designed to give 7,000 power magnification and was good for seeing common bacteria that were about 0.3–5.0 microns in diameter (a micron equaling 1 millionth of a meter) and some of the larger viruses. The scope had a dual viewing feature that allowed two people to view samples at the same time.

Dr. Weiss turned the scope to the highest power and peered at a lung slide from one of the patients with no known organisms.

"This is weird. I see a lot of pretty destroyed alveolar

cells in the patient's lungs and some damaged capillary lining cells."

Rachael turned to Sandy. "What were the hemoglobin levels for these patients?"

"Down to seven or eight versus a normal of twelve to sixteen."

"Pretty low," Rachael said.

"Yeah, you wouldn't expect that with pneumonia or most parasites. And most of them got extra fluid quickly, according to the docs, but still bled out, and 75 percent died right there," Sandy added.

"That's highly unusual for cocci disease. Even the cocci patients that get pneumonia don't have hemoglobins that low. Any common pneumonias in any of these cases?"

"Only a few—two or three at most," Sandy said.

"OK, then . . . I don't know. But we've got to solve this. If it's a new viral-type organism, it will cause a lot of problems. We don't want a repeat of the COVID-19 and COVID-32 outbreaks in 2020 and 2032."

Weiss thought for a few seconds. "We may have to bring in a consultant from the outside," she said.

Dr. Weiss's public health department rarely brought in outside consultants—and then only as a last resort. They were generally expensive, and this year's state budget was tight due to the governor's insistence on no new taxes. All the same, she was determined to solve this puzzle. Three hundred people had already died, and more deaths were likely. As the state public health officer, she was responsible for the health of all Arizonans, and she now felt an overwhelming anxiety since no answers had come from the DNA sequencing.

Dr. Weiss had one other person to bounce ideas off, and that was Dr. Munoz, the federal health officer. Munoz had seen many epidemics in her time and had a very analytical mind when it came to solving epidemiological problems. Weiss called Munoz immediately and briefed her on her observations.

"Any ideas?"

"Possibly a new virus, like SARS-CoV-4," Dr. Munoz said. "With the climate changing drastically, we are indeed seeing outbreaks of new viruses, some mostly or entirely novel. Could be an unknown bacteria. But you said that the sequencing came up with nothing in the NIH database. Is that right?"

"Yes."

"Well, that's impossible. Even if it's a mostly new organism, or mutant, then there should be some similarity to known organisms."

Dr. Weiss looked momentarily dejected.

"So, what are you going to do?" Munoz asked.

"Can you recommend a federal epidemiology expert?"

Dr. Munoz took a few moments to think.

"Well, of course, Dr. Fauci is the gold standard, and it's hard to find anyone else of his caliber now. You'll remember he retired in the late 2020s after receiving the Presidential Medal of Freedom. The country couldn't have gotten through the COVID-19 outbreak without him.

"But we have a great epidemiology expert now who is on his way to becoming another Fauci. I'm thinking of Dr. Jacob Michaels from Harvard. He would be a good match for this problem. I've worked with him before. And some of my staff have worked with him before I came to Arizona. He was involved in the MERS-4 outbreak in Saudi Arabia in 2034 and the recent Ebola outbreak this year in South Africa. Also did some work on Hantavirus in New Mexico last year. He's bright, experienced, and, well, frankly . . . kinda cute. He's around your age too. I think he's at Harvard now finishing a project."

Rachael smiled. Munoz was always trying to find her a husband.

"OK, I'll put in the call first thing in the morning."

DR. WEISS'S OFFICE, PHOENIX

AIR TEMP 115°F, 8:00 A.M.

DR. WEISS CALLED the Harvard T.H. Chan School of Public Health, and after identifying herself, she was put through to Michaels.

"Hello, Dr. Weiss. This is Dr. Michaels. I take it this is about the events happening in Phoenix that I saw on my newsfeed a couple of days ago?"

"Yes. We've come up empty-handed in this outbreak, and you come highly recommended by Dr. Munoz. Dr. Michaels, here's the situation." Weiss didn't like to spend time on chitchat.

"We have some unexplained medical cases here in Phoenix, and we're frankly stumped. I'm sure you've heard about our famous dust storms."

"Sure have."

"Well, a few days ago, about four hundred respiratory patients that tested negative for Valley Fever came to some of our ERs in Phoenix. Most of them presented with bloody cough. The DNA sequences on three-quarters of their nasal and sputum swabs matched nothing in the NIH database. All three hundred of them died, and we don't know why.

"I've exhausted normal avenues trying to investigate this, and meanwhile, it's been on all the news media. The public is panicking, and the governor is all over my case. He's even made funds available to hire a consultant. We need someone yesterday!"

"Sounds intriguing. I'm just finishing a write-up here in Boston on an Ebola project, but I could be on the morning plane tomorrow."

FORTY-NINE THOUSAND FEET OVER EASTERN ARIZONA

AIR TEMP -45°F, 10:00 A.M.

JACOB MICHAELS LOOKED out his window in the new Boeing 888, which had a cruising speed of Mach 1.3, 940 mph. He saw the large, brownish dust cloud hanging over Phoenix. They were about 220 miles out of Phoenix to the east when the pilot came on and said, "Sorry, folks, I'm sure you can see the dust. Even though we have new engines on this plane, they won't tolerate that level of particulate. I'm awfully sorry, but we are diverting to Flagstaff. They recently lengthened the runway, so most of our jets can land there now. I'll give you an update in about twenty minutes."

Michaels's plane landed in Flagstaff in midmorning,

and he quickly went to the rental counter. After a snack, he headed down the 17 toward Phoenix. The new electric Super Toyota hummed along at about 110 on autopilot. The rental car was synched to the magnetic highway on the 17 that elevated the car two inches above the roadway all the way to Phoenix. As a result, Michaels had his hands free. As he looked out the window, he was puzzled.

He had been to Phoenix several times in the late 2020s for conferences. Back then the desert was full of cacti, particularly at about two thousand to three thousand feet in elevation. The famous saguaro cacti liked to live at that elevation. But now, as he stared out the car window, he noticed that they had thinned dramatically from before. And most of those he saw were large, older cacti, a lot of them appearing stressed. Many dead cactus skeletons were visible on the hillsides.

As he approached Black Canyon City, a large, hand-made sign off to the right proclaimed, "Phoenix, 40 miles. Population 925,000. Water—$50/gallon. Limit 4 gallons/day. Gas—$35/gallon. Limit 5 gallons/day. So. You really want to come here?"

He thought the last statement quite amusing—but alarming. In Cambridge, where he lived when he wasn't traveling, the rising oceans had taken most of the lower-lying buildings near Boston Harbor. A large portion of South Boston had become a swamp. However, as far as drinking water supply was concerned, the Boston area had minimal problems, being on the edge of a large northeastern watershed fed by many reservoirs.

Suddenly the car's computer came on, interrupting a Mozart symphony he had called up on Sirius Classical. It said, "Forty-mile envelope: High dust warning—breathing precaution. High temperature warning. Take maximum precautions. Electrolyte solution guidelines recommended. Cooling vests and dust masks recommended."

The warning was ominous. As he approached Phoenix, the visibility was so bad the car automatically put on the low beams and slowed to 45 mph. He glanced at the outside temperature gauge—it read 130°F at 12:30 p.m.

"Holy shit!"

He had worked in Saudi Arabia during the last SARS outbreak, and temperatures had reached 125. But 130 at midday? Boston rarely reached 107 now in the summer.

This was going to be interesting.

Jacob had always been an adventurous type. He would willingly drop everything to go on epidemiological expeditions all over the world. Not only did they supply the experience and excitement he needed in his professional career, but he also loved to travel. And being single, he relished the opportunity to meet new people.

DR. WEISS'S OFFICE, PHOENIX

AIR TEMP 133°F, 2:30 P.M.

"SO, JACOB, how was your trip?"

"Well, as you know, we were diverted to Flag, and I rented from there."

"Yeah, I wasn't surprised when I got your text. The dust here has been unbelievable."

"Yeah, tell me about it!"

As Jacob put down his bags, Rachael couldn't help noticing that he was an attractive man. She had always liked men with goatees. Deisy was right! But Rachael was focused on the task at hand.

"Let's get to it then. Here's what's happened—"

Rachael recounted the major dust storms of July 23 and July 24 and the huge outbreak of coccidioidomycosis during and after the storms, which was expected. She explained to Jacob the sequencing results from her state lab.

"We found a new mutant cocci organism in about 1 percent of the cocci positive patient samples, but the rest matched closely with last year's cocci DNA. I've confirmed that with Dr. Corsini in Tucson, who runs the Valley Fever research lab there. On July 23 at several ERs around the city, and even the next day, July 24, we had four hundred acute cocci-negative respiratory cases. Three hundred of those cases were so severe that the patients died of hemoptysis in the ERs. And At first, we thought we were still looking at cocci, but we double-checked the lab tests. None of those three hundred cases that died matched to any existing organisms on the NIH database—not even a partial match. So you see, it's a mystery."

"And you checked for a new viral pneumonia, COVID-34, Type C Asian Flu, Marburg, Ebola, another coronavirus strain?"

"Yes, all negative."

"What about the path reports?" Michaels asked.

"I looked at them under 7,000 power on our new confocal and saw some unusual destruction of alveolar cells and a large amount of broken, small-blood-vessel cells."

"And they bled out?"

"Yeah. All of them died in the ER."

"Shit. That's a lot of deaths from non-cocci respiratory

cases. I haven't seen such high a percentage of deaths from any of the usual non-cocci respiratory illnesses that I've studied."

"I know."

"Can I see the slides?" Jacob asked.

They went down to the first floor, warmed up the confocal, and slowly reviewed some of the path slides. Michaels was surprised to see such destruction in the lung alveolar cells. They looked shriveled and shrunken, some of them with their cell walls broken apart and some virtually destroyed. And he saw the huge amount of fractured capillary cells supplying the alveoli, just as Dr. Weiss had stated.

"This is really interesting. I've seen something like this with some of the SARS and COVID infections, but this level of alveolar killing is unusual. Is this the highest power available?"

"Yes, here in public health, but we sometimes consult with Dr. McCready, over at the University of Arizona Medical School. They have new scanning cryogenic electron microscopy equipment, just purchased last year, and Dr. McCready is in charge of imaging in the research section. I think he's a polio researcher, if I remember correctly."

"By the way, what were the locations of the emergency rooms where the patients came in?"

"OK, I'll show you."

They returned to Rachael's office on the sixth floor,

and Rachael activated her virtual screen to pull up and map the ER cases and their locations. A holographic map of the Phoenix area appeared in the air in front of them.

Jacob had used these virtual maps in his office in Cambridge before and often found it helpful in plotting outbreak locations for epidemiological studies. As they both studied the virtual map, the ER cases plotted roughly in a line from northwest to southeast, from North Phoenix to the northern edge of Gilbert. Jacob asked Rachael if there were any other unexplained hemoptysis cases anywhere else in the city or county during that time.

She made another request of her computer and pulled up all respiratory cough and hemoptysis cases reported in county hospitals during the dates in consideration. As she explained to Jacob, some of those had been confirmed as cocci-related. Within seconds they were all plotted on the screen.

When Rachael was done, the plot line ran from near Deer Valley, a northern suburb, all the way southeast to Gilbert. There was also a dense patchwork of the known cocci cases covering most of the Phoenix area. The unknown hemoptysis plot line ran through the northern edge of those known cases.

Just then her computer said, "Two more cases in Tucson yesterday—diagnosis hemoptysis, noncocci, unknown organism. Dr. Blanchard reported yesterday, slides taken to pathology at Banner North Tucson. No other cases reported yesterday."

As the voice trailed off, they looked at each other.

"Crap!" Rachael exclaimed. "Now we have some of these cases south of us in Tucson. I think we have a real epidemic. I mean it's spreading . . . and it's not just in Phoenix."

Jacob looked intense. His brilliant mind began to work.

"What about the whole state of Arizona? And has this affected any of your neighboring states?"

"What do you mean?" Rachael asked.

"Well, you have some cases from northern Phoenix, and now one or two in Tucson. There could be others we're not aware of."

Rachael went back to the computer and queried for other similar cases in the entire state over the previous two weeks. More dots appeared on the holographic map, along with case descriptions. The computer announced, "Reported to Arizona Health Services Department: July 14, twenty miles southwest of Cedar Ridge, Arizona, Navajo Nation. Navajo woman, Many Goats clan. Treated in Tuba City ER, expired. Diagnosis: hemoptysis, cocci-negative, unknown cause.

"July 16, Hualapai Village: Hiker taken from Grand Canyon near Hualapai Skywalk. Treated in Banner Las Vegas ER, recovered. Diagnosis: uncertain, hemoptysis, respiratory illness.

"July 22, Lake Havasu City: Tourist drowned in Lake Havasu. Treated in Lake Havasu ER, expired. Diagnosis: hemoptysis, possibly trauma related."

Then, finally, it said: "July 23, Deer Valley. Homeless man fell into CAP canal. Treated in John C. Lincoln ER, expired. Diagnosis: hemoptysis, alcoholic liver disease, possible chronic cocci infection."

The computer plotted four more points on the screen northeast of the previous ones.

Rachael and Jacob both stared for a few minutes at the virtual screen floating before them, trying to digest the information.

"Is that a pattern of anything you're familiar with?" Jacob asked. "What about highways, geological formations, state parks, tourist attractions, airports, rivers . . . anything that might be consistent with these cases."

"Well, most of the Phoenix ER cases run along or near Loop 101, one of the beltways around Phoenix. And one of the cases is close to State Route 95 in western Arizona. However, there doesn't seem to be any consistency between the first case reports, the ones from the Grand Canyon and the Hualapai Tribal Area, and the one in Deer Valley."

"What about reservoirs and lakes?" Jacob asked.

"Aside from Lake Havasu itself, there is one reservoir north of Phoenix known as Lake Pleasant, but it acts more like a recreational area than a reservoir."

"Could there be transmission of, say, a COVID type virus, from one of these recreational areas down highways into the ERs?" Jacob asked.

"I suppose that's possible," Rachael said, "But that

doesn't explain or tie all the cases together, unless they are separate outbreaks, and remember, we didn't see any coronavirus DNA in the sequencing results."

"That's true," Jacob said. He thought for a few more minutes.

"Rachael, just a hunch. Ask the computer to put all of these cases together and see what it comes up with."

"Computer, trace connections among case reports from July 14 to July 27.

"Query: Are there ground, geological, or river tracks that fit case report locations?"

Immediately, a blue line appeared, the line extending from near the Grand Canyon, through Parker, down to Phoenix, and all the way southeast to Tucson. The line mirrored the previous noncocci case line almost identically. The line was identified as the Colorado River and the CAP canal.

Jacob's face lit up.

"So, the computer's saying all of these cases were very near or on the Colorado River or the CAP canal."

"That's right. It seems like it."

"Then we may have a common thread—water."

They both looked at each other. Rachael looked hopeful.

"We've looked at Arizona," Jacob said. "What about other states? It's possible there are other cases out there. What other states are close to the CAP?"

"Definitely Nevada," Rachael said. "Las Vegas, in

particular, has a huge straw into Lake Mead to suck the remaining water from it."

"OK, pull that info," Jacob said.

"It may take a little longer."

Rachael spoke the orders into the computer for similar cases in southern Nevada. Immediately, the answer came back: "Two cases related: July 18 and July 22.

"Case one: Nellis Air Force Base—Pilot expired after crash. Found with blood on visor. Reported to Nevada state health authorities. No organism found. Thought crash related, but suspicious.

"Case two: Banner East, Las Vegas—Cancer patient expired after three days of radiation, surgery, four days of checkpoint inhibitor. Path report showed unusual amount of destruction of alveolar cells, inconsistent with cancer treatments. P- value .002"

"Huh, look at the p-value on the last case," Jacob said. "Extremely unlikely to be related to the cancer treatment then."

As the new cases were read out by the computer, they were automatically plotted on the screen. The blue line now extended through Las Vegas.

"Any common thread?"

"I'm not sure about the cases in Vegas, but Vegas gets its water from Mead, so they could all be water related."

"Yeah. . . . Hmmm." Jacob mused as he sipped his cup of chai. Then his face lit up.

"What if they all were somehow exposed to river water?"

Rachael thought about it for a moment.

"Did you sample for parasites?" Jacob asked.

"Yes, no parasites. And the CAP canal water is sampled twice daily for contamination and nothing has been reported."

"Well, we still might have something waterborne here," Jacob said. He continued: "Could it be something like a new parasite from the fish they use to clean the vegetation in the canal?"

"No, they went to purely robotic cleaners to clean the canal sides years ago."

"OK then. But this might still be waterborne. That may be the common connection."

Rachael nodded. "Seems that way."

"Then let's see the path slides on a better scope." Jacob said. "If it's an uncommon parasite or new virus, then we might need the higher magnification to see it."

"OK, then we'll need to contact Dr. McCready at U of A Bioscience with the cryogenic scanning electron scope. It can get down to the molecular level."

Rachael quickly got on the phone.

"Tanner, this is Rachael Weiss from Arizona public health. I've brought in an expert from Harvard, Dr. Jacob Michaels, an epidemiologist, to look at some path slides. You've probably seen the news about the possible outbreak. Can we use your cryoelectron microscope? We've got some slides that need to be looked at more closely. It's urgent!"

Since it might be a new virus, and virology was his field, McCready was more than happy to comply.

"OK, give me about a half hour to wrap up what I've got on the scope now, and then I'll be interested to see what you've got."

JULY 27

FIRST FLOOR BIOSCIENCE BUILDING, U OF A MEDICAL CAMPUS, PHOENIX

AIR TEMP 135°F, 4:30 P.M.

THE NEW CRYOGENIC electron microscope worked by scattering electrons off the sample, which was cooled to minus 190 degrees C. It was able to get down to nanoscale level, one nanometer being 10 to the minus 9 meters, or one millionth of a millimeter. The scope with the extremely cold temperatures allowed researchers to peer down to the molecular level and was the latest breakthrough in cell microscopy.

Drs. Weiss, Michaels, and McCready were gathered in the scanning cryogenic electron microscope room. Dr. McCready pulled up and prepared one sample from one of the patients who had expired on July 24. Through the multiple viewing ports, they all scanned through the lung sample, finding the alveolar cells. The cells appeared huge in the powerful scope. Many were broken, and some even completely destroyed, similar to what they had seen on the lower-power optical microscope in Rachael's building. But what caught everyone's eye was a group of small, gray-blue objects that seemed to be on or near several of the cells.

"What in the hell is that?" Jacob exclaimed.

Tanner replied, "Not like any virus I've ever seen."

Rachael chimed in, "They look like little crabs!"

As they all gazed down through the scope, something else drew their attention. On one of the tiny gray objects, which was perched on an alveolar cell, they could just barely make out some letters and numbers: NZ2 . . . 7Z. They couldn't make out the middle numerals.

"Holy shit!" Jacob exclaimed. "That ain't made in nature."

Jacob, Tanner, and Rachael continued to stare through the electron microscope at the tiny gray objects. They all seemed to have a peculiar circular shape, which did resemble a tiny crab. Many of the damaged lung alveolar cells had one or two of the objects attached to them, surrounding them, or inside them. A few were also attached to some of the broken capillary lining cells surrounding and supplying the alveolar cells.

As they scanned through other slides from different parts of the lung, they could see the same objects on other alveolar cell surfaces. The objects appeared to have caused similar damage to some of those cells. And it didn't seem to matter which side of the lung they looked at. The group also looked at slides from patients who died on the other date in question. Similar tiny objects were seen on slides from those patients also.

The three of them just stood there dumbfounded for a few minutes, trying to understand what they had just discovered. Then Rachael started speaking.

"We have to find out what these things are and where they came from!" she said.

"Well, obviously they are man-made with those numbers and letters on them. Where did you say these samples came from?" Tanner asked.

"They're from an ER patient who expired with a bloody cough during the dust storm of July 24 and some from patients on the previous day," Rachael said. "And there was no sign of Valley Fever fungus or any other known organism when we matched their sputum DNA with the NIH database."

"Did these patients have any history of medical implants, or were they in any research studies?" Tanner asked.

"Not that we know of," Rachael replied. "But I suppose it's possible."

Tanner had trained on more than a few NIH grants and offered a suggestion. "Why don't you try to contact the NIH Office of Clinical Research in Bethesda?

They would be able to give you a list of current research studies that involve lung implants or other nanoscale experiments. Maybe these patients were involved in medical trials of some sort. These tiny machines, whatever they are, could be some type of medical implant. Medical devices of that scale have been used for some time now."

After thanking McCready for the use of the scope, Drs. Michaels and Weiss went back to Weiss's office. It was 5:30 p.m. Arizona time, and offices on the East Coast would already be closed.

"Would you like to grab a quick bite and then call it a day?" Jacob asked.

Rachael agreed, and the two went to a popular downtown pub near Rachael's office. Rachael had been too busy of late to go out to dinner with anyone, male or female, and was pleasantly surprised at how much she enjoyed Jacob's company. She had asked her network of colleagues about him before he arrived in Phoenix and heard good reports. Even so, she didn't let herself get carried away by his pleasant demeanor.

For his part, Jacob thought he would stay a bachelor forever, but he had to admit that she seemed awfully attractive.

DR. WEISS'S OFFICE, PHOENIX

AIR TEMP 114°F, 6:00 A.M.

RACHAEL AND JACOB PHONED the NIH as soon as they got into her office. It was early morning Washington time when they reached the NIH and described what they had seen on the slides and their hunch that these tiny objects, whatever they were, might have caused the deaths of multiple patients.

The NIH officer in charge gave them the names of ten ongoing research projects using nanotechnology that had started in the last six to twelve months. Some were implants, designed to monitor lab data or metabolism. Others were designed to treat certain diseases. Rachael and Jacob began calling the labs sponsoring the projects.

One project was designed to monitor oxygen levels

deep in the lungs of advanced COPD patients. Another study targeted abnormal rhythm changes in patients at risk for heart attacks and was being conducted at Massachusetts General Hospital. Another was at UCLA and targeted alveolar elasticity changes in asthma patients. Still another project monitored cholesterol plaques inside the lining of small blood vessels. Some studies were already finished, and some targeted patients who didn't match the Phoenix population. On the tenth call, they reached a new startup sponsored by a lab in San Diego.

"Dr. Chris Sorensen, Director of Research. How can I help you?"

"This is Dr. Rachael Weiss and Dr. Jacob Michaels calling from Phoenix. We have been informed by the NIH that your lab is currently using nanotechnology. Is that correct? We obtained your research study number from the NIH today."

Surprised, Sorensen answered, "Well, it depends what you mean by nanotech. We're involved in all kinds of cell biology and genetic studies, but some of our studies are proprietary."

"We understand that," Weiss said. "But what we're calling about has some urgent implications. You see, over the last week in the Phoenix area, about three hundred emergency room patients have died of acute respiratory failure. When we examined the pathology slides of some of these patients under a cryogenic electron microscope, we discovered tiny man-made objects in the nanometer range all over their fragmented lung cells. The lung cells were quite damaged or destroyed, and these machines, if that's what they are, were imprinted with the letter-number combination NZ2 and then something that we couldn't make out, perhaps three other numbers, and then 7Z. "

There was a long silence on the other end. Sorensen recognized the partial number sequence but waited to hear more.

"We have already ruled out nine other labs that are doing nanotechnology research. No one else has used these sets of numbers from the NIH."

"And what kind of problems did you say these small objects are causing?" Sorensen asked, although he had already heard and understood Dr. Weiss's explanation.

"When we examined the pathology slides of alveolar cells from the deceased patients, we saw widespread cell damage and some of these tiny gray-blue objects attached or surrounding the cells. And as I said, this partial letter-number combination, NZ2 . . . 7Z, could be clearly made out on the side of most of them."

"Huh. Why are you so sure these came from our lab?"

"We're not. But your lab fits the profile. We've called all labs with studies sponsored by NIH and currently using this type of technology in the last six to twelve months."

"What about other private labs?" Sorensen asked.

"None doing this now. At least not with NIH money."

A funny feeling began to creep into Sorensen. He recognized that the numbers matched, at least in part, their grant numbers. But he wasn't sure how and what Dr. Weiss was describing could even be possible.

"You know, even if some of this is true, and I'm not sure it is, it would be impossible for our research to impact any patients in Phoenix. At this very moment, the president of our corporation, Dr. Jeremy Stone, is in Denver working on a clinical research project there. And the project has barely begun. It's got to be some other lab.

"Dr. Stone arrived in Denver about two weeks ago and has been there the whole time, so I don't know how we could possibly be involved. It's absolutely impossible!

"And anyway, I can't divulge any information about our research. This area is highly competitive now. And proprietary," Sorensen added. "You'd have to speak to our corporate lawyer, and he's on vacation now for two weeks."

"And you don't have any clinical research projects here in Phoenix?"

"No, absolutely not! We are just working on laboratory experiments that would never leave the lab."

"Well, even so, we may want to contact Dr. Stone. Could we have his number?" Rachael asked.

Sorensen paused a moment. All sorts of thoughts churned through his mind. He didn't like the direction of the conversation but felt obligated to comply. As he reluctantly gave them Stone's contact number in Denver, the funny feeling in the pit of his stomach intensified.

DR. WEISS'S OFFICE, 9:00 A.M.

"Dr. Jeremy Stone. Who's calling?"

"Hello, Dr. Stone. This is Dr. Rachael Weiss and Dr. Jacob Michaels in Phoenix. We got your contact number from Dr. Chris Sorensen at your lab in San Diego."

"What's this about? I'm a busy man!"

Nothing annoyed Stone more than interruptions in his research, especially when he was involved in new experiments.

"Are you presently involved in clinical research with nanotechnology?"

"Who did you say you are?" Stone asked angrily.

"Dr. Rachael Weiss. I'm the public health officer for the state of Arizona, and Dr. Michaels is on loan from Harvard. We've been looking into some patient deaths in ERs in the Phoenix area over the last week or so. We are investigating the possibility that your lab may be involved somehow in these deaths."

"What? I've seen something on my newsfeed about some unknown infectious agent in Phoenix, but that would have nothing to do with my lab. That's preposterous!" Stone now felt an enormous anger surging through him.

"Well, we looked into the labs in the US that are presently involved in trials using nanotechnology, and your lab is the only one that matches the information we have."

"And what information is that?" Stone was becoming really irritated now.

He put down the iPad he was reviewing that held patient labs.

"We have four or five machine numbers on what appear to be man-made objects found on the lung cells of deceased patients here in Phoenix that match the NIH project grant number given to your lab. We have already contacted the appropriate NIH research division and confirmed this."

"What? What do you mean you found numbers that match?"

"We could see through a very powerful cryoelectron microscope that each tiny object had the partial letter-number combination NZ2 . . . 7Z imprinted on it."

"And these objects caused enough damage to kill patients?"

"Yes."

"Are you sure these objects are machines and not viruses or bacteria? From what I heard on the newsfeed from Phoenix, it's more likely a virus or bacteria."

"No, we've had a virologist look at them. Plus, as I mentioned, they appear to have some sort of writing on them."

Stone had recognized the partial study numbers of the nanobots he was using, but he automatically rejected any possible connection to what they were telling him.

"I don't see how my lab could be involved. I've been in Denver for the past two weeks, and even if I did have some type of machines capable of treating patients, they would all have been with me here in Denver."

Stone was loathe to give out any information about his research project, having been burned many times in the past by laboratory leaks to other researchers. He had always been highly secretive when it came to his research.

"Can you think of any way that these machines could have come into contact with patients here in Phoenix?" Rachael asked.

"No. Like I said, the research trial is here in Denver. I oversaw the first injections just two weeks ago. And I don't recognize those numbers!"

But even as Stone finished answering, a vague feeling of uneasiness came over him. He couldn't believe that these two had found some of the research numbers on his project. Slowly, his mind went back over two weeks ago, when he had stood on the edge of Horseshoe Bend watching his travel pack fall one thousand feet to the river below. He had seen one of the torn bot packs floating away from him. Could the bots have gotten all the way to Phoenix? But how? Even if the bots went down the river, most of them would probably have washed to the shore or sunk to the bottom by being in the water. He hesitated on the phone for a moment, unsure of what to say.

"No, simply impossible," Stone said. "You must have the wrong research number. Maybe the NIH gave you the wrong number. Or maybe it's some other private lab you want. Maybe some medical device company. Listen, I've got to go. I'm already late for a meeting here."

Rachael and Jacob had picked up the unease in Stone's voice.

"Well, we may want to recontact you with further questions."

"Ah . . . I'm quite busy here. Could you wait until I return to San Diego?"

"Dr. Stone, people have died. This can't wait."

"I see. Well, I'm sorry, but I won't be reachable for a few days. I'm the principal investigator, and I'm too involved here." Stone hung up.

Jacob got right to the point: "Either the bastard's lying, or we need to start looking for another lab."

"Yeah, but we don't have much time for that. Other patients may be dying as we speak!"

"Yeah," Jacob said. "What do we know about Stone?"

"Well," Rachael said, "he's one of the guys who won the Nobel for defining the minimal base sequence for a living organism. And, therefore, brilliant. But I've also heard rumors that he's a ruthless competitor when it comes to scientific research."

"Yeah, makes sense," Jacob said. "Hey, you know, my stomach's growling, and we've been at this all morning. How about an early lunch, and we'll decide on our next steps."

Rachael picked a new chic restaurant in downtown Phoenix for the meeting. After they ordered, she again bypassed chitchat and got right to the point.

"Jacob, what do you think our next move should be? It

seems like Sorensen and Stone may be holding out on us."

"I would agree," Jacob said. "Sometimes you need to call in the lawyers. I've found this helpful in past investigations. And this definitely involves federal research money. I'm thinking we should contact the FBI in San Diego and get them involved. We may also need a judge to subpoena the Stone Lab or Sorensen, and then we'll be able to confirm or not confirm that Stone's lab was involved."

"OK. Sounds good. I like the idea of involving the FBI. We'll call San Diego after lunch."

Now that a plan was in place, Rachael felt more comfortable loosening up a bit. She told Jacob about her scientific interests and how and why she had decided on a career in public health. Jacob reciprocated and told Rachael about his travels around the globe conducting research and offering assistance whenever the latest outbreak struck. He was barely out of college when COVID-19 hit in 2020, and he had been somewhat undecided on a specific interest area, but the enormity of that pandemic, and the lingering effects that had lasted well into the 2020s, had cemented his interest in epidemiology. Jacob explained to Rachael that after college at Harvard, he had taken a year off to work as an intern with a World Health Organization epidemiologist in Africa who was involved in a project to eradicate polio. He had traveled to Africa with the WHO team, working in their field lab and helping to conduct polio vaccinations in villages over most of southern Africa. That experience had been a good one and had whetted his interest both in epidemiology and world travel. When he returned to Cambridge, he applied for the Doctor of Public Health program, finishing early in 2024. After that, as he explained to Rachael, he was involved in epidemiological research projects all over the world, including new MERS and COVID outbreaks. During that time he had published several papers on epidemiological methods and had developed quite a reputation as a world-class field and quantitative epidemiologist.

After Jacob's stories, Rachael reciprocated with her academic and work history. She told Jacob that since she was a young girl, she had always been interested in science and the workings of the natural world. Later, in college, she had become interested in the health of populations and had pursued her Doctor of Public Health degree in Baltimore at the Bloomberg School of Public Health.

When she came to Phoenix in early 2021, the city was still in the throes of the COVID-19 outbreak, and she had then gained a lot of experience in the modeling of viral outbreaks.

The two of them also shared their interests in traveling, and particularly hiking and spending time outdoors. Rachael was surprised to hear that Jacob was interested in astronomy, and she shared her similar interest, describing many trips to Kitt Peak in southern Arizona to peer through some of the large telescopes there.

By the end of their lunch together, they were both

pleasantly surprised by how much they had in common. They began to feel a growing bond between them.

After lunch, Jacob and Rachael returned to her office to contact the regional FBI office in San Diego. They explained the situation and the need to involve them. They told the agent assigned to the case why they had reason to believe that the Stone Lab was the one that produced the machine in question and discussed the evidence they had accumulated so far.

The agent agreed on the possible need for a warrant. She said she would like to meet with them in person in San Diego the next morning to gather all the facts. Rachael and Jacob booked a morning flight to the coast for the next day.

BANNER DENVER WEST, RESEARCH DIVISION

AIR TEMP 110°F, 11:30 A.M. MST

AFTER STONE FINISHED the call with Weiss and Michaels, he tried to think of any possible scenarios in which his nanobots could have infected patients in Phoenix. He again rejected the possibility of the bots that fell into the river at Horseshoe Bend causing any problems. Even though the bots were tiny, it seemed unlikely they could navigate all the way to Phoenix. It had to be something else. Did someone steal some from his travel pack before it fell into the river? Maybe that waitress he had sex with at the Canyon. Could she have given it to her professor in Flagstaff to experiment on patients? She had seemed awfully interested in his project. It was a definite possibility. She could have gotten up and stolen some while he slept. He would never know.

What about some other researcher trying to get back at him for past misdeeds? Maybe. His paranoid mind considered this. But who? And how could they have gotten ahold of the bots? Or maybe one of the kids in the lab in San Diego stole some! He would have to get Sorensen to check the new hires out again. Had he fired any of them recently? Yeah, that made a lot of sense—disgruntled young punk fired by Nobel laureate's lab steals his latest work.

You had to be ruthless to survive in scientific research, and Stone had not been above pushing ethical boundaries in his career if it could help him get ahead. He had never stolen another scientist's work, but he had thought about it. Yes, it had to be one of these scenarios, most probably the stupid punk stealing them. But even so, why would the bots be attacking perfectly healthy patients?

Stone decided he would call Sorensen the next morning and discuss all of this. He needed to get back to his work and pushed all these thoughts into the back of his mind for the time being. But that night he dreamed of tiny nanomachines crawling into his lungs and attacking his cells.

It was a restless sleep.

JULY 29

STONE LAB, LA JOLLA

AIR TEMP 97°F, 8:30 A.M.

SORENSEN WAS IN HIS OFFICE early the next morning when Stone called.

"Good to hear from you, Jeremy. How is the trial going?"

"Well, actually it started OK, but I'm puzzled about something. We have three groups in the trial as you know. There are two control groups. The first control group has been treated with standard treatments: radiation, surgery, and chemo. The second control group is cancer-free, but has been infused with the same number of nanobots as the treatment group, just to make sure the body can clear them from circulation and as a double check for any side effects. The treatment group, of course, has gone through standard treatments also but has received the nanobot infusion. The controls and treatment group are all the same age and matched in all details. We're only sixteen days into the trial, but already we're beginning to see some unusual effects in one of the control groups."

"What do you mean?" Sorensen asked, concerned.

"Well, a small number of the cancer-free controls have started to have some mild cough with reddish-brown mucus. It's concerning. Not something we expected. And most of those with the cough have slight fevers, like colds or other mild illnesses. Came down with them after the trial started."

"Really?"

Sorensen listened intently. He was always the go-to man in the lab for problem-solving.

"And you're sure the mucusy cough wasn't simply from hard coughing or throat irritation?"

"We don't think so. These control patients without cancer are really healthy."

Sorensen considered this for a few moments.

"What kind of fever did these controls have?"

"Nothing much, maybe a degree or two at most."

"Huh. . . . By the way, I got a call yesterday morning from two scientists in Phoenix, a Dr. Weiss and a Dr. Michaels. They are investigating an outbreak of unexplained hemoptysis in respiratory patients in Phoenix. Seems that about five to six days ago they had some kind of an epidemic in their ERs all over the city."

"I know. They called me too," Stone said. "But I told

them I didn't think our research had anything to do with it. The patient deaths they were describing were all in Phoenix. Anyway, they could only make out part of the numerals on the nano-sized objects they were looking at."

"Yes, that's right." Sorensen pondered. But his mind was already theorizing and extrapolating.

"Have you kept the experimental machines with you at all times?"

"Yes. . . . Of course! But . . . well—"

"But what?"

"Well, I didn't tell you, but half of the nanobots were lost when I was photographing Horseshoe Bend on July 11. A stupid girl taking a selfie knocked them off the cliff where I was standing, and they fell into the river below. I had somehow forgotten to take the bots out of the pack that held the camera gear."

"What? Are you kidding me?"

Sorensen began to feel the same uneasiness as the day before.

"No, it's true," Stone admitted. "But remember, I had half of them in the briefcase, so we still had enough to do the trials."

"How many?"

"About 200 billion. The other half in my briefcase were with me all the way to Denver. By the way, I want you to double-check the background on all the postdocs again. And have we fired anyone recently?"

Sorensen ignored Stone's comment about the lab

personnel. "And were the bots you lost encased in the cooling pack that I gave you?"

"Of course! But they fell one thousand feet, and when I went with the helicopter below to look for the pack, I saw that the pack had disintegrated and was floating down the Colorado. So maybe the cooling pack containing the bots disintegrated too.

"I just couldn't get to it. It was floating away too fast. And I thought nothing of it . . . until now. I figured the damaged pack and the bots would sink to the bottom, wash onto the shore, or at least be trapped by the big dam near Vegas. Even when those people called from Phoenix yesterday, I thought it would be impossible that our lab was involved. I was thinking through this last night, and I think the only logical explanation is that some kid in our lab stole them." Stone didn't want to admit to Sorensen the other possibility he had considered—that the waitress at the Canyon had stolen them.

The phone fell silent for a few seconds while both minds considered the evidence that had been presented to them and explored all possible scenarios.

Finally, Sorensen asked, "And even if they got through the dam at Vegas, how would they ever reach Phoenix?"

"I don't know. I don't see how," Stone said.

Another long pause.

Sorensen did a quick calculation in his mind. He was unbelievably good at such things.

"You know," he said, "The weight of one of those

machines is just 1.2 picograms. One trillionth of a gram."

"Yes. What are you getting at?" Stone asked uneasily.

"Just that . . . is there any possibility—" Sorensen began.

"That they could have gone all the way to Phoenix and could still be functional?" Stone finished the sentence for him. "How would they, how could they, if they traveled down the Colorado River? Doesn't it end in Mexico or somewhere?"

Sorensen pondered this. He had lived in Phoenix briefly twenty years ago—and suddenly a frightening thought popped into his head. Oh shit! The Central Arizona Project. It goes from the Colorado down to Phoenix and ends in Tucson. But it's got to be nearly two hundred miles to Phoenix!

Sorensen did the calculation in his head. After a mere fifteen seconds, he had the answer.

"At 1.2 picograms, approximately 19.4 percent of the bots . . . could theoretically make their way to Phoenix down the CAP canal. That's about forty billion of them."

"OK. But even if we assume they could still function after so much time in the water, how could they make normal people sick? They're designed for non- small cell lung cancer patients," Stone said.

"I don't know. We designed them specifically to attack cancer cells." Sorensen pondered a few seconds more.

"Let me review all the experimental and animal data again. I'll see if there is any reason this might happen from the data. Then I'll get back to you."

"OK, and do it quickly," Stone ordered. "I don't like those people asking questions."

"I know. Me neither."

Stone hung up the phone, and as he did, that sense of uneasiness, that funny feeling in the pit of his stomach, intensified. He felt sick. He now identified a new feeling: fear.

STONE LAB, LA JOLLA, 11:00 A.M.

Sorensen glanced at the virtual newsfeed that he had called up in his office. He saw a taped interview with Weiss from the day before.

"Dr. Weiss, have you made any progress in this investigation? You've confirmed that three hundred patients have died from an unknown outbreak, right?"

Weiss looked totally exhausted.

"We're doing everything we can. We've got an outside consultant from Harvard here in Phoenix working with us."

"Do you think this could be connected to the recent SARS B outbreak in Indonesia?"

"Probably not," she replied. "We haven't found any evidence of that. But we're looking into a lab in San Diego that may be involved."

"Can you tell us the name of the lab?"

"Not at this time."

Sorensen breathed a sigh of relief as he watched Weiss walk away to escape the reporters. At least the lab wasn't on all the newsfeeds yet. But he wondered how long it would be before some reporter came snooping around. He turned off the feed.

Sorensen had spent most of the morning reviewing the project data on the nanobot. Next, he wanted to talk to all the staff before taking a break for lunch. He called in all the researchers who had worked on the project. As he began questioning them, he got to Noah Sanders. Sanders, age twenty-four, was just out of a master of science program in biotechnology at UCSD. He reported directly to Sorensen.

"Noah, when you did the original animal work, did you find any unusual problems with the machine? Anything at all? I remember that all of your reports and quality control summaries were signed off as nominal."

"Let me think," Sanders said. "Why is this important now? Dr. Stone is already doing the clinical trial in Denver, isn't he?"

"Yes, and he is having some issues, some slight brownish-red mucus coughed up in one of the the control groups. We've also been contacted by public health authorities in Phoenix about some deaths in respiratory patients in their ERs over the last week that they can't explain. Seems like they have traced imprinted letters and numbers on nano-sized objects back to our lab. So we need to find out if there were any problems with our machines that could explain this."

Sanders hesitated. As a recent hire, he knew he was still under probation.

"If I tell you something, will you have to tell Dr. Stone?"

Sanders idolized Stone and, like all the young scientists in the lab, wanted to please his boss. He was also afraid of him, having witnessed his temper on several occasions.

"Depends on what it is," Sorensen answered warily.

Sanders paused a long time.

"There was something... but I didn't report it because I thought it didn't matter in terms of the human experiments. And I didn't want to disappoint Dr. Stone. I know how important this project is to him."

Sorensen felt the sinking feeling again in his stomach.

Sanders continued, "When we did the later experiments on the monkeys, I noticed something interesting. When I did the calculations for the affinity of the binding sites on the bot, it appeared that if the temperature of the bot itself was elevated a few degrees, even just 1.8 degrees Fahrenheit above normal body temperature, then the binding site affinity for *normal* lung cells increased markedly, I think by 65 percent at least.

"But I didn't include it in the write-up, again because I didn't think it would matter for the cancer-cell binding, which was the main focus of the research, and normal cells don't usually heat up like the tumor cells. So I kept quiet. I didn't want to disappoint Dr. Stone."

Sorensen was stunned. He put his head down on the table and muttered some swear words. His mind went immediately to his last conversation with Stone, where Stone had described the abnormal slight hemoptysis in the cancer-free control patients who had had fevers. He quickly realized they now had at least a hypothetical explanation for how the bot could attack normal lung cells. But what about the ER patients in Phoenix?

Even if some of them had slight fevers, that information still couldn't explain so many deaths, certainly not the three hundred that had been reported over a few days. He was furious with the young researcher.

"Do you realize you may have caused a serious problem?"

"I'm sorry . . . really sorry. Am I going to be fired?"

"I'll have to talk to Dr. Stone about that. As for now, you're off the project and out of this lab. But don't leave town. I may want you to talk to Dr. Stone."

Sanders slunk away back to the lab to collect his things.

Sorensen had to think about how he was going to present this information to Stone. Stone would be furious. After a long while, he dialed Stone's number.

"Jeremy, we may have a problem," Sorensen began. "Remember that new intern from UCSD?"

"Yeah."

"Well, I've just spoken to him. Seems he's been holding some data back from us."

"Christ! What the hell is it? Did he steal some of the bots?"

Sorensen then explained what Sanders had just admitted to him about the binding sites.

"That could explain why you're seeing some extra mild hemoptysis in those cancer-free control patients in the trial, especially the ones who had colds or minor upper respiratory infections with the mild fevers."

"Damn it, Chris!"

Sorensen could hear the anger beginning in Stone's voice. The cursing continued a little longer.

"All right," Stone finally said as he digested the new information and began to think. "But how do we explain as many as three hundred ER patients in Phoenix dying in one or two days?"

Sorensen had already thought about that.

"Is there any way the temperature of the nanomachines could have warmed the 1.8 degrees? What about the bots that went into the river?"

"I don't see how," Stone answered, exasperated. "There's no way!"

They both fell silent, each man to his own thoughts.

Stone's mind again went back to the day standing above Horseshoe Bend. He put himself back in the helo, descending into the canyon and seeing the dead woman below with the blood leaking from her head. He saw himself walking along the riverbed, then wading into the water, then swimming, trying to reach the pack and the nanomachines that were slowly being carried away by the current. And then it came to him.

It was the river. The goddamn river! He thought to himself.

"Chris, I may have an explanation," Stone said quietly after he had calmed down a bit. "When I was trying to reach the nanobot container floating down the river, the water seemed awfully warm, about body temperature, I would guess. At the time I didn't give it much thought. I knew that it must have warmed some with the hot weather. But now, I'm wondering if it could have warmed enough to somehow activate the bots and increase the binding on normal cells. Is that even possible?"

Sorensen considered what he had just heard. Again, some quick ideas came automatically to him.

"Jeremy, what was the air temperature the day you lost your pack?"

"I think it was at least 130 degrees Fahrenheit."

"Wow! And you said the water felt maybe as warm as normal body temperature?"

"Yeah, possibly. Or warmer. It was pretty warm. Almost felt like a bathtub."

"Then, according to Sanders, it would have taken only another 1.8 degrees to activate the increased binding to normal cells.

"Jeremy, is there any way that the river temperature could have gotten one or two degrees higher during the time the bots went down the river into the CAP canal and on into Phoenix? Of course, this assumes those tiny machines would have escaped all the dams along the way."

Stone thought about what Sorensen was proposing—that an error in the bot production may have made it prone to bind to normal lung cell membranes when its temperature was elevated by as little as 1.8 degrees. And add to that the possibility that the bot could have warmed another degree or two as it made its way down the Colorado and on into Phoenix. But that would have to mean that many highly unlikely events would have all needed to occur at the same time.

Stone knew that a series of highly unlikely events were sometimes what propelled research and caused scientific breakthroughs. And catastrophes. And if it was the latter, that would mean something else. It would mean that, as the principal investigator for the lab, he might be responsible for the deaths of three hundred people.

"Jeremy, uh Jeremy, what are you thinking about?" Sorensen asked, trying to get Stone back into the conversation.

"Oh . . . I'm just trying to figure out if this is even possible."

"OK . . . OK. And what do you think?" Sorensen asked. "We still have to explain how the bot could have warmed 1.8 to 2 degrees Fahrenheit on its way down the river."

Stone felt that queasy feeling again in the pit of his stomach. In his mind, he went back to the days prior to arriving at the dam site in Page driving his Super Prius, and back to what the weather service was warning about at the time: an unusual, super-high-pressure area that would progress east across Arizona and into New Mexico, raising air temperatures to extremely high numbers.

"Chris, wait a minute. I remember now . . . there was an unusual high in the area at the time that might have raised the air temperature another 10 or so degrees. Would that be enough to raise the river water the 1.8 degrees required to activate the nanobot binding?" Jeremy asked.

"Give me a minute or two," Sorensen replied. "I'm going to have to do some tricky calculations."

"OK."

Sorensen entered the ambient air temperature numbers into his watch, along with the bot's dimensions, weight, and composition, the formula for the 1.8-2.0 degree Fahrenheit warming of a body of water, the sun's angle at that time of year, the width and average depth of the Colorado from Page to Parker, the average depths and widths of the CAP from Parker Dam to Phoenix, and the average flow rate of the river and of the CAP canal. He punched the calculation function.

In two seconds, the answer came back. The voice from his watch slowly read the answer: Calculations conclude that probability of a 1.8 degree Fahrenheit rise along this course is 91 percent with a p value of .04.

Sorensen came back on the phone. "There's a 91 percent probability that it's possible."

"Holy shit! Do you know what this means?"

"Yeah. We're in trouble."

"Yeah." Stone paused a moment, and then continued. "Chris, I know we've worked together for a long time. And I value your contribution and all of your experience. Your loyalty too. I need to think about this for a while. I need some time alone." A plan was forming in Stone's mind even as he spoke.

"Try to hold off the people in Phoenix for as long as you can," Stone instructed. "I'll text you a number where you can reach me. I'll transfer control of the Denver trials to you."

"But," Sorensen began, "what if they conclude it's our lab?"

"You can handle it. You always have."

"Well then, what are you going to do? Are you going somewhere?" Sorensen was incredulous. What was Jeremy thinking?

"I'll be in touch." Stone clicked off.

Sorensen felt a deep wave of fear. As head researcher in Stone Lab, he knew that if this panned out, he might be implicated also. He had a lot invested in the twenty or so years that he had worked with Jeremy, including the Nobel. But, now, he found himself weighing his options.

They might be able to put off the investigators for a while, but not forever. And since the NIH was involved, they could possibly lose any future funding.

He had to weigh his loyalty to Stone alongside his own future. And if he was drawn into the investigation, as was almost sure to occur, then . . . would he even have a future in research?

It occurred to him that possibly he should contact the FBI immediately. At least then they could see that he was cooperating. But that would be admitting guilt. Maybe there was still some other explanation for the deaths in Phoenix, but Sorensen knew in his years of experience and in his heart that all the data pointed to only one reasonable conclusion.

After a while, he made a decision. He would wait, at least until the investigation was further along, and see if they definitely confirmed that the Stone Lab was involved.

JULY 29

FBI DISTRICT OFFICE, SAN DIEGO

AIR TEMP 106°F, 11:30 A.M.

"HELLO, I'M SPECIAL AGENT BERGER. Thanks for coming out here. What can you tell me?"

Rachael and Jacob brought her up to date on the evidence so far.

"As you can see, we have every reason to believe that this particular lab, the Stone Lab here in La Jolla, constructed a research machine of nanometer dimensions that bore the partial letter and number sequence NZ2 . . . 7Z and therefore, may be implicated in sickening and killing three hundred patients in Phoenix from July 23 to 24.

"We have this nanotechnology grant number from the NIH Office of Research. The problem is that the lab, or should we say, the scientist there in charge, Dr.

Sorensen, refuses to confirm this. We've already spoken to him by phone. Another interesting fact—it seems that the principal investigator, Dr. Jeremy Stone, also refuses to answer any questions. So we need to get in there and review their research files to nail down whether they, in fact, have produced this machine."

Berger replied, "OK, I've got the warrant in hand. It came in from Judge Rodriguez early this morning. Here is the plan. We're all going to be wired. The microphone is tiny, almost a nanomachine itself—1/1000 of an inch in diameter. When we get to the lab, let me do the initial talking. Let's head out."

STONE LAB,
LA JOLLA

AIR TEMP 108°F, 1:00 P.M.

THE STONE LAB OVERLOOKED one of the prettiest views of the Pacific Ocean and was on multimillion-dollar real estate. Sunlight glinted off the glass windows of the lab buildings, which were perched on top of a cliff. It was a warm day in San Diego, but nothing like the day Rachael and Jacob had just left in Phoenix.

In the old days, prior to global warming, it was unusual for the temperature in San Diego to rise above 83 degrees in the summer. But now, 113 was not unusual. However, San Diego leaders had been smarter than those in Phoenix in one regard. They had begun construction of a desalinization plant early in the 2010s, and it was finished in 2015. A second was constructed in 2023. The plants now supplied about 65 percent of the municipal water needs. A third plant was nearing completion.

Rachael, Jacob, and Agent Berger entered the lab and encountered the receptionist, who dialed Sorensen's extension and announced, "The FBI is here."

Sorensen had just finished his call with Stone. How could the FBI be here already! He felt that his loyalty to the lab and Jeremy required that he stay and talk to the agent.

Sorensen made his way through the lab and out into the reception area. He recognized Weiss from her recent interviews on the newsfeed. He had also seen Michaels interviewed multiple times over the years whenever the latest pandemic struck. The African American woman standing with them must be the FBI agent, he thought.

He spoke carefully to the three visitors. "Hello, I'm Dr. Sorensen, Director of Research here. How can I be of help?"

Agent Berger pulled the warrant out of her briefcase for Sorensen to see and said, "We have a warrant here to inspect your research files. We are looking for the following NIH research letter-number combination: NZ2, missing 3 middle characters, and ending in 7Z. Are you in possession of this number on any of your research trials?"

Sorensen said, delaying, "I . . . I'm not sure. . . . I don't think so. But you came to inspect the files, so I'll access them. Please follow me back to my office."

Once all four were in his office, Sorensen closed the door and called up the complete research data from the lab's main computer. They appeared virtually in the air in front of the group. The front page of each was titled "Research Project." They were organized in numerical order.

"As you can see, we have all of the research files in the computer, so you should be able to look through them," Sorensen offered.

Agent Berger and Drs. Weiss and Michaels began to scan through the extensive data files. After twenty minutes, they finally came across the study they were looking for.

It was titled: "Research Project #167—Nanobot clinical trial of non-small- cell lung cancer in adults forty to sixty-five. NIH project #N2035–NZ23657Z-RSC#3."

Jacob enlarged the data and began to read. The description of the entire project was there from inception to design to manufacturing of the nanomachine, along with dimensions of the bot, immunological studies, materials used, production time, production schedule, statistical computations, likelihood of cancer cure, Phase I and Phase II trial summaries, and on one of the last pages, the letter-number combination stamped on each of the nanomachines: NZ23657Z, which matched, except for three numbers, the initial lettering and numerals found on the patients' path slides.

Agent Berger called Sorensen back into the room. He had been out in the lab trying to get some work done and waiting for the inevitable. Berger spoke first.

"This data indicates that your lab designed and produced tiny nanomachines capable of treating lung cancer patients. They were each stamped with the letter-number combination NZ23657Z. Can you confirm this?"

"Ah . . . well . . . yes," Sorensen said, hesitatingly letting the words come out.

"Then explain this machine to us," Rachael said, "and how it could possibly end up causing so many problems in Phoenix."

Sorensen explained the project from the start: "The initial idea was vetted in 2033, but production didn't begin until the lab had enough money. You see, the lab is partially financed by private equity. People who believe in high tech solutions in health care, cancer in particular. . . . So production began in late 2034 and finished in 2035. The initial machine was designed to inject a highly lethal peptide directly into lung cancer cells after the machine had become bound to the surface of such cells in non-small cell lung cancer patients. We had gotten permission from the NIH to begin a phase III clinical trial in a Denver hospital owned by Banner Health."

Jacob broke in. "Any way this could have killed three hundred patients in Phoenix emergency rooms?"

Sorensen delayed answering again for a moment and then decided on his course of action.

"No, I don't believe so because Dr. Stone had taken the machines to Denver personally in his car to start the clinical trial. So I don't know how they could have caused any problems in Phoenix. But then, I've already told you that."

"Dr. Sorensen," Rachael said, "as we told you on the phone, we have found the partial letter-number combination NZ2 . . . 7Z on what appear to be nano-dimensional machines all over the destroyed lung cells of patients in Phoenix. This matches the specific NIH grant number that your lab received in 2035. We know this from the pathology slides that we reviewed."

"Really?" Sorensen tried to feign disbelief. "But the machines were used in Denver, not Phoenix. Maybe the machines were designed by another cancer lab and used on patients in Phoenix," he said. "We've been racing two other labs for the design. One in Boston and one in LA."

"We already looked into that. The timing and type of research is off," Jacob replied. "A lot of those studies have finished."

"Well, we also wondered if one of our young scientists stole some of the bots. You know how competitive scientific research is. I'm in the middle of questioning the staff about that and reviewing personnel records. Other than that, I don't know how—" Sorensen replied, feeling the sweat start to break out on his face.

"OK. We'd like to contact Dr. Stone again. He hung up on us before. Do you have his cell number?"

"No, I don't."

"Are you sure?" Berger pressed.

"No, I really don't. He told me he was leaving the

lab for a few days to attend to some personal matters. I believe he has a relative who died suddenly," Sorensen said, expanding on his lie.

"Hmm." Berger said, studying him closely for any tells. "Well, as you know, as principal investigator, he is ultimately responsible for anything your lab produces. And of course, you, as head of research, would also be responsible."

"Yes, of course." Sorensen was really getting nervous now, and sweat poured from his forehead.

"Dr. Sorensen, don't leave town. We will want to contact you again. We're done here. We need to find Stone."

As Weiss, Michaels, and Berger left the lab, Berger said, "We'll check the airlines out of Denver International. If he left in a hurry, we'll find him on a manifest. We could also check his recent credit card charges."

"Good idea," Rachael said. "What about his cell phone usage or car rentals in Denver?"

"Oh, of course, all of that," Berger said. "Don't worry, the Bureau is very experienced at tracking people. We'll find him. Even so, based on Sorensen's reaction, and the data we found, we already have our answer. I personally don't understand how these bots could have gotten to Phoenix, so I'll leave that to you scientists to tell me how that could have happened. Or we'll eventually get it out of Sorensen."

"Yes, I agree," Jacob said. "I've known Chris Sorensen for many years. He's supposed to be as brilliant as Stone.

I have a feeling he's already figured it out. He seemed pretty nervous to me."

JULY 30, ICELANDAIR FLIGHT # 1324, 53,000 FEET OVER NEWFOUNDLAND, 3:00 A.M. NDT

"Good evening, passengers. From the flight deck, this is Captain Hilsedottir. We are at eighteen thousand meters over L'Anse aux Meadows, Newfoundland, where, experts say, my ancient Viking relatives established the first settlement in America."

Stone noted the Icelandic accent of the female pilot.

"Estimated time to Greenland, 1.1 hours, and Reykjavik, 1.8 hours. Airspeed Mach 1.3."

Stone reclined in Saga class. He had just awakened from the recurring dream in which tiny black machines attached themselves to his lungs, causing them to bleed.

A soft voice speaking perfect English said, "Hello, sir. Would you like some coffee, chocolate, or skyr?"

Barely awake, Stone chose the coffee and pondered his future.

DR. WEISS'S OFFICE, PHOENIX

AIR TEMP 120°F, 9:00 A.M.

"DR. WEISS, I just got a push alert on my cell you'll want to see. Take a look!" Sandy said.

"*Breaking News*—Nobel laureate Dr. Chris Sorensen fined $5 million and given jail time for his part in the nanobot debacle that killed three hundred in Phoenix in the summer of 2036. Nobel withdrawn. Dr. Jeremy Stone, founder of Stone Lab, the company that made the defective bots, has also been fined and given jail time in absentia. Stone initially fled to Iceland. The FBI thinks he continued on to Eastern Europe soon after and continues to live there under an assumed name."

Rachael dialed Jacob in Boston.

"Jacob, have you seen the news?"

"Yeah, I got an alert on my phone."

"Wow, they really threw the book at Sorensen!" Rachael said. "And they still haven't found Stone!"

"Yes, and look at the damage his lab caused," Jacob replied. "All those people who died in Phoenix."

"Stone was an idiot to try and carry billions of nano-machines to Denver in his car. He should have known better," Rachael said.

"I know. And what about that young researcher in his lab, Sanders, or whoever. I think he bears some of the responsibility. He kept information from both Sorensen and Stone."

"Yeah . . . and Sorensen claimed that neither he nor Stone were to blame since Sanders kept the information from them. Sorensen tried to get off the hook by saying it was all an unfortunate accident."

"And what about Stone's ego? He seemed uncon-cerned about the deaths of 300 people," Jacob said.

"Yeah. He disappeared."

"And what about the climate change that tripped it?" Jacob asked.

"You mean the unusual ten-degree temperature ele-vation from the high-pressure system that went through the region back then?"

"Yes, but you know . . . this may not be the last 10 degrees in temperature elevation due to global warming. Here we are two years later, and the drought shows no signs of ending," Jacob said.

EPILOGUE

NO NEW CASES of unexplained hemoptysis were reported in Arizona in 2036 and future years. But going forward, Valley Fever cases continued to spike with the inevitable dust storms.

In absentia, Jeremy Stone was barred from doing any further research with the NIH, and his Nobel was withdrawn, but he was completely unconcerned about his fall from grace. He had relocated to Reykjavik, Iceland, and worked as a genetic researcher there at an offshoot of ReCode Labs. He had managed to completely change his identity, and "Jeremy Stone" no longer existed. He had followed Sorensen's trial in the US and was amused to learn that the FBI thought he was in Eastern Europe.

In Iceland, the climate had warmed to such a degree that winters were no longer snowy, and the summer sun rarely peeked from the clouds. The country's official bird, the puffin, had gone extinct, a victim of the declining supply of its food, sand eels, because of warming waters in the North Atlantic.

Stone never returned to the US. He died in 2039 from a fall into a crevasse on the largest glacier in the land, Vatnajokull. Glacial melting had allowed him hiking access.

Sorensen got ten years of jail time and used the time to write his memoirs. He hoped that sales of the book and speaking engagements would help him pay off some of the fine he had been assessed and his legal fees. He also continued to appeal his case, arguing that he had been merely following orders from Stone and that Sanders had withheld crucial information.

Noah Sanders was so ashamed of his error that he committed suicide in late 2036.

After enduring several years of a long-distance romance, Jacob the confirmed bachelor finally settled down and married Rachael the confirmed bachelorette in 2039. The couple settled in Boston. Jacob received the Lasker Award in medicine in 2039 for his work in epidemiology on Ebola and the nanobot crisis. Rachael accepted a teaching job at the Harvard T.H. Chan School of Public Health and worked as a consultant for WHO, sometimes traveling with Jacob.

After the manufacturing mistake was discovered, Stone's phase III trial in Denver was halted and then terminated by the NIH. The trial was never finished. However, in 2038, shortly after Sorensen's conviction, a group of researchers from MIT succeeded in showing that non-small cell lung cancer could be treated safely and effectively with nanomachines.

Sandy Morrison got her PhD in 2038 and continued working at the Arizona Department of Health Services. She had become intrigued by the evolution of mutations in cocci and coronaviruses. One day she hoped to become the director of public health.

Lake Mead reached deadpool in 2038, and all flow into the CAP ceased.

The southwestern drought dragged on another ten years, well into 2048, and showed no sign of ending.

Except for a few resilient folks, most of the people of central Arizona, like the Hohokam before them, were forced to pack up and leave. Their only record would be 240 miles of empty, crumbling CAP canals that lined the Sonoran Desert west of Phoenix, accumulating dust. Atop where the old canals once stood, a few hardy lizards could still be seen doing their pushups while trying to attract mates and basking in the early morning heat . . . only a few signs of the unending ego and hubris of man remained.

ACKNOWLEDGMENTS

THIS WOULD NOT HAVE BEEN the same book without the knowledge and unending support of my wife, Barbara, who spent many hours reviewing drafts and giving advice and suggestions.

Many thanks to my cousins, Lisa Wolf Johnson and Mary Klinkel for early manuscript reviews and helpful suggestions.

Thanks to Malik Toms and Beth Staples, two professors associated with the Virginia G. Piper Center for Creative Writing at Arizona State University.

A special thanks to Harry Singer, a member of the Navajo Nation, who was most generous with his time spent reviewing the Navajo section and teaching me some Navajo words.

Many thanks to my friend Andy Koffmann and his wife Lynn Rickert, who both read sections of the manuscript and offered suggestions.

Special thanks to my copy editor, Tom Locke for his beautiful editing, and the team of self-publishers at My Word Publishing, especially publishing consultant Polly Letofsky, cover designer and layout person Victoria Wolf of Wolf Design and Marketing Inc.

Special thanks also to Caltech, which launched me on my scientific career.

ABOUT THE AUTHOR

JEFF LARSON is a physician/scientist who obtained both his MS degree in genetics and cell biology and his MD at the University of Minnesota. He originally trained as a scientist at Caltech, where he got his BS. He has published in *Science*. Jeff's research interests are bio-engineering, nanoscience, and genomics. He currently teaches at the University of Arizona Medical School and studies the effect climate change is having on water supplies in the Southwest. Originally from South Dakota, he now lives in Phoenix with his wife Barbara and several hummingbirds. *The Last Ten Degrees* is his first novel. Visit his website at www.JeffLarsonAuthor.com.

Made in the USA
Monee, IL
20 February 2021